MIDNIGHT

PROMISE

D1521704

MIDNIGHT PROMISE

ARC Shifters

By

Julie Trettel

Midnight Promise
ARC Shifters: Book Three
Copyright ©2019, Julie Trettel. All rights reserved.
Cover Art by, Logan Keys of Cover of Darkness
Editing by, Beth Culver

Thanks and Acknowledgments

To all those people out there just looking for their tribe, a place to fit in. This book is for you!

And to my tribe of authors: Heather Karn, Jennifer Grey, Char Webster, Nicole Kelley, Melanie Gilbert, and Nicole Zoltak, along with so many more who help me along the way and still more I meet each and every day. Thanks for always having my back! Love you guys!!!

Jade
Chapter 1

"Greek Row is going down!" I exclaimed to the small group that had shown up to discuss the rally. "Since the beginning of Archibald Reynolds, those elitist pricks have segregated themselves from the rest of us as they sit up in their fancy houses and throw elaborate, invite-only parties. This is the twenty-first century. We are striving for an inclusive society, which goes against everything the Greeks stand for. It's time we rise up and let them know exactly how we feel. Now who's with me?"

I looked around at the pitiful group I had to work with, only seventeen people had even bothered to show, and of them, only a few raised hesitant hands. I had spent hours handing out flyers and taping them to every dorm room on campus. It was hard to keep my disappointment in check at the lack of support for something I was so passionate about.

"With your voices, you guys. Let me hear you. Who's with me?"

To her credit, my friend Melissa cheered loudly, but she was the only one. A couple others made a noise at least, though one of them may have just farted. I couldn't tell for sure. Sometimes I felt as though I was the only one who even cared.

I couldn't stand elitists. I was a coyote shifter, and my entire life had been spent with others looking down their noses at me. Why? I was a good person and I would never harm anyone, but coyotes were considered the lowest on the totem pole of canine shifters, and other shifters were quick to remind me of that, and then try to put me in my place. That was why I hated the Greeks. They reminded me of every stuck-up shifter who thought they were better than me just because of the species of spirit animal within them. Well, that was bullshit!

A guy at the back of the room raised his hand, and it gave me hope for our school.

"Yes?" I asked enthusiastically.

"The flyer said there'd be food. How much more do we have to listen to before we get to eat?"

And just like that, my faith in humanity, particularly shifter-kind, crashed and burned.

"Snacks are on the table. Help yourself," I murmured.

Suddenly the room was alive with excitement as they all rushed towards the refreshments I'd set out, took their fill, and left.

Only three remained with me, including Melissa.

"I'm sorry Jade. I really thought we'd have more support from the student body," Melissa said.

"The Greeks can all go to hell," one of the girls said. "Sorry. I'm still just so pissed with them. Especially Delta Omega Gamma."

We all nodded. "They're the worst," the other newcomer admitted.

"I'm sorry, what're your names?"

"I'm Kaitlyn," she said.

"I'm Violet," she said rolling her eyes. "Yes, thank *Bambi* for that. I'm a skunk shifter and my mother thought it would be cute. It's not cute. I was going to change my name when I turned eighteen, but when I mentioned it, Mom was so devastated I couldn't go through with it. Oh, and I'm told I'm an over-sharer, so it's okay to just tell me to shut up if I talk too much."

Melissa and I shared a quick look.

"It's nice to meet you both. Thanks for sticking around and supporting us. I'm very passionate about this subject, as you can probably tell. I'm Jade, and this is my friend Melissa."

"Do you really think it will work?" Kaitlyn asked. "I mean, taking on the Greeks. What do you hope to achieve by it?"

"I hoped more people would care, for one," I said. "We live in a society that says they want equality, yet they aren't willing to fight for it. Today's turn out proves that."

"I think people in general want acceptance more than equality. They want to feel like they belong to something bigger than themselves. That's the appeal of the Greeks," Kaitlyn said.

I rolled my eyes. "What about individuality? I want to be accepted as much as the next person, but I want to be accepted for me, the real me, not some fake me that I pretend to be just to fit in."

"Some of us are just too scared to show the real us," Violet offered.

"You say that, yet you came right up and told us you're a skunk shifter," I pointed out.

She shrugged. "Just cause I've learned to come to terms with it and would rather be upfront than waste my time on fake friends, doesn't mean others feel the same. I mean I do understand the appeal of the Greeks. I just wish they were more inclusive for parties and didn't do dumb shit. I heard the doghouse puts on a dog show every year where they make their pledges bring an ugly girl to a party. The uglier the "dog" the better."

"I heard they weren't doing that this year," Melissa piped in. "It backfired on them last year."

"Really? How?" Violet asked.

"Well, according to my friend, none of the pledges understood the meaning behind the dog show. All but one stole actual dogs from nearby houses and the winner brought his girlfriend who happened to be a wolf shifter. Get it? A dog. Anyway, Ember says they aren't even bothering with it this year. She's engaged to one of the brothers of Delta Omega Gamma."

"You're friends with a D.O.G.?" I asked feeling a little disgusted at the thought. Why hadn't Melissa mentioned that sooner.

She shrugged obviously feeling my disappointment. "I don't really know him well, just his fiancé, Ember Kenston."

"Wait, like Emmy Kenston? Alicia Kenston's daughter?" Violet asked and she shrieked when Melissa nodded. "Wow! That's so cool. Boy did they cause quite an uproar around campus last year when Alicia Kenston showed up here. I mean, I don't think anyone knew Emmy even went to school here, or that she was a shifter. I've seen her around campus a few times and she does seem nice."

Melissa smiled and I could tell she really liked her friend Ember. "She is."

I was going to have to tread carefully around that one. If Melissa was that close with Ember, then she wasn't really against the Greeks as much as she let on. Ember Kenston screamed elitist.

It was my senior year, and this was going to be the legacy I left behind. I wanted to see the Greeks crash and burn so badly that it often kept me up at night.

My freshman year I'd been the dog asked to a party by a cute boy I had been crushing on, and thought he really liked me. Turned out the joke had been on me and I'd never forgotten how horrible that realization had made me feel. No one could really understand it, and now it was payback time.

It wasn't that I was ugly. I knew that. I just looked different and I liked it. My eyebrow, nose, lip, tongue, and belly button were all pierced, along with several holes in each of my ears. I liked to change my hair color regularly, and although they weren't visible, I had three small tattoos.

My mother liked to say I was born into my rebellious stage and just never outgrew it. While it was true that I rarely gave a shit what anyone thought of me, there were moments in my life when I had cared. I had even vowed that things would be different at the ARC, maybe not my looks or my preferred choice of black or dark clothing, but I would open up and try to fit in. That had lasted right up until the dog show, a whole two months of freshman year.

"I've met Ember, she really is sweet. She and Chad are the cutest couple together," Kaitlyn added, jolting me from my jaunt down memory lane.

"Chad, he's one of the D.O.G.s?" I asked.

Kaitlyn and Melissa both nodded. I pulled out a notebook from my backpack and quickly wrote down the connections, not saying another word about it. I didn't miss the worried look they shared.

"So, votes for Greek council will be coming up this week. Do you guys know enough about them to guess who may be voted president this year?" I asked.

"Brett, for sure," Kaitlyn said. Something in her voice almost sounded proud of that.

"Who's Brett?" Violet asked.

"President of the D.O.G.s," I added with a hint of disgust. I knew the name and that was enough to ensure I couldn't stand him.

Kaitlyn had a worried look on her face, but she didn't comment further. There was something about her that seemed off, but I had a natural gift for understanding people, almost like a sixth sense, and my gut told me she was a good person. I couldn't help but like her.

We weren't really making any progress with this meeting. The entire day had been a wash, and I still needed to find a way to reach the mass of students and get them fired up about taking down the Greeks.

"I think I'm going to call it a day and go get some lunch," I said.

"I'm starving," Kaitlyn said.

I hadn't planned on inviting anyone along, but I didn't have a good reason to say no either as she invited herself.

Melissa gave me a quick hug and said she would pass on lunch but call me later. Violet followed her out and suddenly it was just me and Kaitlyn.

"I, uh, I was just going to the café," I admitted.

"Great," Kaitlyn said completely unaffected.

We walked the short distance to the café in comfortable silence. Coyotes liked their space, but we also did well with non-threatening females, and my animal within displayed no fear towards my new friend.

We went our separate ways to select our food, and I checked out and sat down first. I looked around and didn't see Kaitlyn anywhere. I was a little disappointed, assuming she had ditched me, but it happened often enough that it only bothered me a little.

I shrugged it off and started eating. I jolted in surprise when a tray dropped on the table across from me and Kaitlyn slid into the booth.

"Oh, I thought you had changed your mind," I said.

She snorted and grinned. "You're not getting rid of me that easily. The pizza looked old and kind of nasty, so I waited for a fresh one to come out of the oven." I nodded that I understood. "So, Jade, what are you majoring in?"

I smiled and relaxed again. "Pre-law."

Kaitlyn rolled her eyes and laughed. "I really am not surprised to hear that whatsoever."

I shrugged. "It suits me well."

11

I was proud of everything I'd accomplished. I may not look like the stereotypical law student, but it didn't take people long to recognize the fire that ran within me. Coyotes tended to be nocturnal, so the long late hours of my internship over the summer hadn't bothered me one bit. I had quickly made a name for myself with the firm I'd been assigned to, and I couldn't wait to graduate and begin the next phase of my life in law school.

Brett

Chapter 2

I heard the front door of the doghouse open and close. The catcalls from the living room followed by laughter told me she'd finally arrived. I was more than a little irritated that I hadn't heard something sooner. It was late in the afternoon, and the meeting had been scheduled for ten in the morning. I couldn't imagine what had taken her so long.

I waited in my room at my desk pretending to study. The door swung open without warning and Kaitlyn walked in. She closed it behind her and then walked over and sat on my bed pulling her knees up to her chest.

"Well?" I finally asked when it was clear she wasn't going to be forthcoming about what had happened.

Kaitlyn shrugged. "I like her."

I rolled my eyes. "You like everyone," I pointed out.

"I know, but I really like her, Brett, and she has some valid points. I'm still not sure what happened to make her hate us so badly, but I'm certain there's a story behind it all. And I'm going to find out what it is."

"And how exactly do you plan to do that?"

She shrugged again. "Befriend her?"

I laughed. Kaitlyn was a sweetheart, and my brothers and I would protect her with our lives, but we both knew she stunk at keeping female friends. The only reason she ended up in Theta was because they promised her a room to herself. The sisters of Theta liked Kaitlyn's connection to the doghouse, and so it was a mutually beneficial situation. Sure, she liked her sisters okay some of the time. Other times, she would hide out in the doghouse for weeks just to stay away from them, but that was Kaitlyn. She would always get along with guys far easier than girls, so the idea of her befriending Jade, who was proving to be the biggest pain in my ass possible, was comical.

Kaitlyn threw a pillow at my head. "I'm serious, Brett. It's weird, but we like connected or something. I get her and I really like her. I think she liked me too."

"Until she finds out you're a Theta girl, then you instantly become enemy #1."

Kaitlyn sighed, and I could see I'd hit a sore spot. "Maybe I can get her to come around before that happens."

"Really? You're not just teasing me? I mean this bitch has stirred so much shit that the administration is taking her accusations seriously."

"Don't call her that, Brett. You don't even know her."

"I've seen enough on her report to know her type," I pointed out. I'd had a full investigation run on Jade Michaels right after the bitchfest I'd had to endure with the administration last week.

I hadn't wanted the position of president of Greek Row. It wasn't even public knowledge yet that they'd voted me into the job and already I was being called in to deal with this. I had my hands full enough as president of the doghouse. I certainly didn't need anything more on my resume, but when Ayanna, president of the stuck-up, exclusive panthers was the only one to step up for the position, everyone turned to me for help and I'd caved. Now I was stuck with it for my entire senior year.

I had been blindsided by Jade with her accusations of Greek Row not living up to the inclusion policies of the school and the dream held by our founder, Archibald Reynolds.

I wanted to retort that if that had been old Archibald's dream, then why had he originally opened it as a wolf shifter exclusive college? He had a choice and he'd chosen exclusivity, not inclusion when he'd originally opened the school.

It was roughly a decade ago when a grad student had stumbled across a box thought to have once belonged to Archibald in an attic of one of the oldest buildings on campus. In the box was a journal containing notes he wrote all about his wishes for the school to be inclusive and celebrate all of shifter-kind and not just the wolves.

For me that had been a godsend as it opened all sorts of opportunities I otherwise wouldn't have had. I certainly wasn't against inclusion as this Jade chick seemed to think. As president of Delta Omega Gamma, I felt like I'd done a lot already to unify the sorority and fraternities and I was proud of that. I didn't like hearing the accusations this girl was spouting and I didn't want her to get away with continuing to do it.

Kaitlyn had agreed to go in undercover and get the scoop for me.

"So, how many people showed up anyway?" I finally asked.

She sighed. "Not nearly enough. I felt bad for Jade. There was a couple dozen that showed up, but they were only there for the food. Once she weeded those out, there were only four of us left, and that's including me, Jade, and her friend Melissa, who's friends with Ember, by the way. So, one."

I laughed. "One? That's it? Geez. Why is the administration up my ass over one little person?"

"I'm telling you, Brett, Jade isn't a bad person. You'd probably even like her. She's female and she happens to be cute," Kaitlyn teased.

"Are you saying I have no other standards than her being female?"

She gave me a look that said "Duh!"

I shook my head in disgust. "I've seen pics, she's a freak just wanting to cause trouble as her legacy before she leaves this place."

"She's not a freak," Kaitlyn said sternly. I wasn't used to her coming to the defense of anyone like that. It was weird.

"Don't tell me you drank the Kool-Aid while you were there," I joked.

"Be serious for once, will you? I like Jade. She had a lot of valid points, and so did Melissa and Violet."

"Who's Violet?" I asked.

"The one. Keep up already."

"What are these valid points then?" I asked only trying to humor her.

"Your stupid dog show for one," she said.

"I ended that already," I said. I had always thought it was a horrible idea. I hated how they essentially degraded women for a laugh like that, but I was overruled by those calling it tradition. When it backfired on us last year, I used it to effectively end the old tradition. There would not be anymore dog shows in the doghouse.

"I know you did, and we discussed that too," she admitted. "I know you aren't a bad guy. I know a lot of the Greeks aren't bad people or think they're better than everyone else. Okay, a few legitimately do, but not the majority."

"I agree, and a lot of the parties here are open access. I mean when was the last time we threw an exclusive party? I can't even remember, and only on special occasions. Otherwise, the more the merrier."

"I know. I'm a Greek too, remember?" she asked sarcastically.

"I do remember. Do you?"

Kaitlyn huffed. "I know who and what I am, Brett. I also stand by what I said. Jade is a good person. She's just passionate about her beliefs, and I really think there's a story behind it all. I mean she really hates us. There has to be a reason and I'm going to find out what it is and make it right."

"I hope so. When's this big rally of hers anyway?"

"I don't know yet. I don't think a date has been set." Kaitlyn stood and stretched. "I'm heading home. I'll keep you posted."

"Thanks," I said honestly. I knew how loyal she was and if she felt this strongly about the girl, then it was killing her inside to play double agent spy like this.

I tried not to let the guilt of it affect me after Kaitlyn left. I knew it wasn't right to put her in this position, but now that we had an "in," I was optimistic that maybe I could fix it before things really got out of control.

I still couldn't believe Kaitlyn thought I'd like this girl. I picked up the picture of Jade taken her freshman year and examined it closely. She had piercings all over her face and her hair was a bright red, though everything else about her from her clothing to her makeup was black.

I glanced into the mirror that hung over my dresser. Blonde hair, close shaven, and bright blue eyes stared back at me. I was wearing a navy polo and khakis. I glanced back at the photo of Jade and laughed out loud. Nah, she had to have been messing with me.

I threw the picture back into the folder of info I'd collected on Jade and shoved the whole thing into a drawer, then I got up and headed for the common room.

"'Bout time you showed your ugly face around here," Jackson said. "I'm about to start another round, want to join in?"

He held a game controller towards me, but I declined.

"Come on, wolfhunter247 is kicking my ass. I need backup."

"Let Tyler play with you," I suggested.

I couldn't tell if the kid was glad I'd suggested him, or ready to murder me in my sleep for it. He was often hard to read, but surprisingly after the fiasco during his pledge period, Tyler seemed to fit right in. Begrudgingly or not, he took the controller and sat down to play.

When Tyler first pledged last year, he was dating Karis, who had turned out to be Damon's one true mate. We almost didn't give Tyler an invite to pledge because of the conflict it caused, but he had graciously backed out of the equation when he realized what was happening. Damon and Karis are happily mated now, and Damon, being the ass he can sometimes be, still likes to terrorize the kid over it.

Chad came out of his room to join us.

"Hey man, do you know a Melissa? I think she's a friend of Ember's," I asked.

"Melissa? Yeah. Ember was going to room with her last semester before all the shit went down with her old roommate and all that fell through. Sweet girl."

I rolled my eyes, sick of hearing about how great these girls were. They weren't sweet or great, they were evil and trying to destroy our house.

"What was that look for?" he asked.

"Nothing. Just struggling with the concept of "sweet" you and Kaitlyn seem to have today," I grumbled.

"Did she get the scoop on the infamous Jade for you?" Jackson asked without taking his eyes off the screen.

"Something like that."

All the brothers knew I had been obsessing about Jade since I was presented with the first flyer. Dozens of them had been handed

17

to me before the event this morning. She had to have posted thousands of them. I wasn't even sure we had that many students at the ARC, but those ugly yellowish orange bright pieces of paper seemed to be everywhere around campus.

"Uh-oh, doesn't sound like it went all that well," Chad observed.

"What happened?" Jackson asked.

"Kaitlyn found a new best friend," I said through gritted teeth and headed back to my room before they could even respond.

Jade

Chapter 3

The week passed by uneventfully. The only thing out of the ordinary for me was the constant presence of Kaitlyn. It felt like she was going out of her way to befriend me. What probably bothered me the most was that I really liked her too. She was easy to talk with, smart, and funny.

We had at least one meal together every day and made plans to see a movie in town on Friday night. I was looking forward to it. I didn't have a lot of girlfriends, and this year I didn't even have a roommate to pretend I had a friend to hang out with. It was nice to have a real friend.

"Hey Jade," Kaitlyn said as I stepped out of my last class on Friday. She surprised me with a big hug.

"Hey you. I thought we were meeting later."

"Yeah, but I got tied up in my last class and am still around, obviously. Want to grab dinner out before the movie?"

I genuinely smiled. "Sure, that sounds great. Can we swing by my room so I can drop off my bag and change real quick?"

"Absolutely. Lead the way," she said.

Kaitlyn followed me across campus to my dorm. She looked around my room as I grabbed a change of clothes from my closet and headed for the bathroom.

"Make yourself at home," I hollered over my shoulder before closing the door.

I was an only child, but if I'd had any sisters, I would have wanted them to be just like Kaitlyn. She was dressed in a cute little sundress for the evening and I decided dressing up would be fun. Of course, mine was just a little black dress because that was my thing.

The two of us were like night and day, Kaitlyn was full of life and all sunshine, and I was as dark as night and well, not full of sunshine. We made quite the awkward pair.

When I came out of the bathroom feeling cute, I suggested we go to the steakhouse in town just up the street from the theater. Kaitlyn looked a little uncertain but agreed.

"It's good, I promise."

"Can you drive?" she asked.

"Sure," I said, grabbing my purse and keys.

On the drive to the restaurant, Kaitlyn seemed preoccupied as she frantically texted someone.

"Is everything okay?" I finally asked.

She sighed but smiled back at me. "It's fine. Family can be a pain in the ass sometimes."

I shrugged. "Wouldn't know. Don't have any. I mean, sure I have my mom, but it's always just been the two of us. No siblings."

She frowned. "What about your pack?"

"Coyote, not wolf, remember? While most do mate for life, like any other shifter, we tend to keep to ourselves. My dad split the second he found out Mom was pregnant with me. I guess he's out there somewhere, but he'll never be family. They weren't true mates. If I ever find my true mate, I'm not sure what I'll do. Didn't exactly have the best role models for that."

"What? That's so sad, and lonely," she said.

"It is what it is. Just the nature of the beast and how we're created."

"I'm not sure I believe that," she said.

I laughed. "That's because you're a wolf and all about community and family and stuff."

"Fine, but that's not a bad thing. Just because you don't have much biological family, doesn't mean you can't create your own."

I shook my head at her tenacity as I parked, and we walked into the restaurant.

"Kaitlyn!" the host exclaimed the second she walked through the door. "Haven't seen you around here much lately. How are you?"

"I'm good. This is my friend, Jade. Do you have an open table for two?"

"For you? Always. Right this way," the host said. "I'll put you in Damon's section," he said with a wink.

"Thanks," she murmured.

"There's a line outside waiting to be seated," I loud whispered after we were seated. "How did you do this?"

She shrugged. "I used to eat here a lot."

We both cracked up laughing. I knew that wasn't entirely it, but I was hungry and not complaining.

"Hello ladies. I'm Damon. I'll be your waiter this evening. What are we drinking tonight?" the waiter said as he stopped by our table. My stomach churned and I fought the urge to vomit. I hadn't seen Damon Rossi since freshman year. He was the number one culprit behind my desire to take down the Greeks. Asshole.

"Just water for me," I said sourly.

Kaitlyn scrunched up her nose in disgust. "Merlot for me, please."

I hadn't considered Kaitlyn's financial status may be well above my own. I took for granted that all college students weren't struggling and paying their own way like me. I had lucked into enough grants to cover all my expenses and even a little extra to help with living expenses. Combined with the wages I'd earned interning over the summer, I was very well-off heading into senior year, but not to drink merlot and dine on steaks in a nice restaurant on a regular basis well-off. I had suggested this place as a special occasion. I rarely ever ate off campus.

Damon didn't say another word as he turned and left to fetch our drinks, returning quickly.

"Do you ladies know what you'd like to eat? And are we celebrating a special occasion or something?" Damon asked.

Kaitlyn sighed. "Damon, this is my friend, Jade. Jade, this is Damon." *Wolf,* she mouthed in explanation and my stomach lurched as I fought not to bolt.

"Nice to meet you Damon. Do you go to the ARC?" I asked. Kaitlyn shot me a look of concern as I knew my voice was strained.

21

He shook his head. "Graduated last spring. My uh, girlfriend, is a sophomore this year so I'll be sticking around until she graduates," he explained, and I knew he really meant his mate.

I couldn't believe Damon had actually settled down and taken a mate. It had rocked the entire campus the previous year. But what I really couldn't believe was that he didn't show one single sign of recognition towards me.

"That's sweet," I managed to say. "Oh, and I'll have the six-ounce sirloin," I added, choosing the smallest steak on the menu and therefore the cheapest, and hoping that my quick order would get him the hell away from me.

"You sure you don't want a bigger one?" Kaitlyn asked, but I shook my head. I'd be hungry again later, but it was enough to get me through the evening first.

"I'm sure. Baked potato loaded, and the seasonal veggies please."

"Got it. Kait?"

"The same I guess," she said.

"Kaitlyn, get whatever you want," I said. "What would you normally order?"

Damon laughed and she punched him in the arm playfully.

"I'm saving room for popcorn. We're going to a movie tonight."

"Sure, okay. Two sirloins, rare?" he asked.

"Is there any other way?" I asked.

He grinned. "I like her. So, two sirloins, rare, with baked potatoes and vegetables. Anything else?"

We both shook our heads. I was still in shock by his words. He likes me? What the hell?

"It's weird you know. I bet you know every. . ." I hesitated and looked around the room. We were off campus and the place was likely filled with humans. No one was paying any attention to us, but it wasn't something you just blurted out either. "Wolf," I finally managed in a low voice. "I bet you know all of them. I mean, I know there are others like me around campus, but I don't actually know any of them." It was true. There were at least a dozen coyotes currently attending Archibald Reynolds, but I didn't know a single one.

"That's kind of sad. I mean, I know everyone from my, uh, family, that attends. We're sort of close like that."

That must be nice, I thought. I'd never had that kind of comradery. Family was nothing more than my mom for me. I didn't care about any of the coyotes around campus, let alone even bothering to get to know them.

Wolves were different. They needed that closeness. They needed their pack. It was natural that they would seek each other out.

I shrugged. "It's just different for me, I guess."

We moved on to happier conversation discussing the mundane things in life, like how cute the lead actor is from the movie we were about to see. We laughed and I even giggled a few times while we waited for our meal. Who was I?

For some reason I felt lighter and happier whenever Kaitlyn was around. She often carried this second smell that I adored. I kept meaning to ask her about it and where she bought it. Usually I couldn't stand perfumes.

Damon finally brought our meal along with two of the biggest steaks I'd ever seen. They definitely weren't the six-ounce ones we ordered, but I saw the stare down from Damon and watched as Kaitlyn rolled her eyes. Instead of fussing, I cut into it and took a big bite. It was the best thing I'd eaten in a long time. Damon left with a satisfied smiled and I moaned through each bite as Kaitlyn teased me.

"I have a confession to make," Kaitlyn said as we were finishing up.

I felt nervous waiting for whatever she was about to share. Kaitlyn in one week had quickly become the best friend I'd ever had.

"What is it?" I asked.

"I don't do well with other girls. Most of my close friends are guys. I mean I have friends, or at least people that would call me their friend, but I don't usually make an effort to get to know other females. I'm not sure what it is that makes you different, but I can honestly say you are the closest girlfriend I've ever had."

This should have been good news, but she looked sad saying it.

"Is that all? I thought it was going to be something bad. It's probably not a big shocker, but I don't make friends easily either-period." I knew there was something more to it, something she wanted to say but for some reason was holding back.

"Can I get you ladies anything else?" Damon interrupted.

I looked up just in time to see the look he shot at Kaitlyn. Her body stiffened then she sighed in resolve. I had a feeling whatever the real confession was, I wasn't going to hear it tonight.

"Just the check," I said and even managed to give him a smile without gritting my teeth.

Damon stared at me like it was the first time all night he was really seeing me. His eyes went wide in surprise and I knew he finally recognized me, too.

He shook his head. "Um, dinner's on the house tonight, ladies." He smiled toward Kaitlyn, then back at me. "Enjoy the rest of your evening."

"Seriously? Why?" Kaitlyn asked.

Damon shot her a look to shut up.

"Can't I just do something nice for once?" he asked.

"You really don't have to," she insisted.

"I really do," he said sounding almost apologetic as he stole another glance my way.

Brett

Chapter 4

The front door burst open a little after one in the morning. Damon walked in and immediately began pacing the common room. Jackson grumbled when he passed in front of the TV.

"Do you mind?" Jackson asked. "I'm about to obliterate that asshole once and for all. Wolfhunter247 is going down!"

"That's all you ever do these days," Tyler grumbled.

"What's up Damon?" I asked. It was clear something was bothering him.

"It's all my fault," he blurted out.

I looked up at my friend wondering just how much he'd had to drink.

"Don't look at me like that. I haven't had even a sip of alcohol. I'm serious here, man. All of this shit you're going through with the administration is my fault."

"Fine, I'll bite," I said, still not certain he was telling the truth about drinking. "How is this mess your fault?"

"Jade," he said.

"What about her?"

"Have you met her?"

"No, why?"

"Do you remember our freshman year? When we pledged here?"

"Of course, I do."

"Remember the dog show that year?"

I thought back but couldn't. I shook my head.

"He wasn't here," Jackson spoke up. "Dammit! He won again," he cursed, throwing the controller across the room and turning his full attention towards us. "Brett was out of town that weekend. I don't remember why, just that he wasn't there."

"Right, that's the weekend my nephew was born, and I went home," I said.

"Okay, well, tonight Kaitlyn brought that Jade chick into my restaurant for dinner. They were going to a movie or something. Girls' night out."

"Kaitlyn's still hanging out with her, why? I mean I know she's trying to get me some info on her, but dinner and a movie on a Friday night? That's way more than I'd ever ask of her."

"Missing the point here," Damon said as he continued with his story. "They came in and I met Jade. She looked a little familiar, but I couldn't quite put my finger on it, then it dawned on me. The dog show! Jade was my dog freshman year. I'm the reason she hates Greek row so bad she wants to shut us down completely." He sat down on the couch next to me. "I'm sorry, man. I screwed up."

We all knew Damon had been a womanizing asshole for much of his college days. It wasn't until he met his true mate, Karis, a year ago that he started to change. He didn't even remotely resemble the man he had been before Karis.

"That wasn't your fault. You were just playing along with the pledge rules, D. Don't sweat it. I'm sure that's not the only incident of failure Jade's faced in her time here. I've seen her pictures and all those piercings and dark makeup. She's a freak," I said.

"Dude, not cool. She seemed, I dunno, nice. It was good to see her and Kaitlyn laughing and whispering. It's the girliest I've ever seen our girl. She looked happy, Brett."

I sighed. "I noticed that last weekend right after they met. I told her to pull out and forget it, but obviously she didn't listen. Kaitlyn's been avoiding me all week."

Jackson got up and retrieved his controller and sat back down. "If Kait likes this girl, then she's okay. I trust her instincts better than my own when it comes to defining people like that."

"But if Jade's righteous stand is correct, where does that leave the doghouse?" I asked.

The room went quiet. No one had an answer for my question, not even me. I didn't want to hate a total stranger, but I was also very protective of my family, and the doghouse was my family. Now, as leader of the Greeks, I felt they were all my responsibility, too.

As the silence started to become awkward, I stood and walked out, and then down the hall to my room. No one followed.

I didn't have all the answers. I felt bad about having Kaitlyn sneak around behind this girl's back, but I needed to understand what I was dealing with. I didn't like being blindsided.

I changed into pajama bottoms, turned off the light and went to bed. I stared towards the ceiling into the darkness.

The room lit up as my phone rang. Grabbing it off my nightstand I rolled my eyes and groaned. it was after midnight, but even though I'd been at the ARC for the last four years, my mother still couldn't understand time zones. I swiped to answer.

"Hey Mom."

"Oh good, you're still awake. Your father was just yelling at me for calling so late. You know I can never keep your time straight."

"I know, Mom. What's up?"

"You sound stressed. Are you okay?"

"Mom, I'm fine. What's going on?"

"Nothing. Does a mother need a reason to call her son?"

"After one in the morning, yeah, usually," I teased.

"Well, sometimes I just want to hear your voice and make sure my baby's okay."

"Mom, I'm fine. There's just a lot going on here."

"Tell me. I'm a good listener."

I sighed. "Okay, so there's this girl here. Her name is Jade, and she's taken a personal vendetta against the Greek system here. As you know, I'm the president of all Greek Row so it's sort of my responsibility to protect all the houses, meanwhile she wants to take the whole system down, crying for inclusion and whatnot."

"What is her spirit animal?" my mother asked.

"How am I supposed to know? Does it matter?"

"Well, sure it does. I mean we're coyotes, Brett. You know what sort of negative stigmatism that carries. We have to rise above people's perceived notions to get ahead in life, something your wolf friends wouldn't understand. Maybe this Jade feels left out and so she is speaking out for equality. You of all people should be able to appreciate that, son."

"Brett, this is your father." Great, I thought. They put me on speaker phone once again. I wasn't sure why it still surprised me or bothered me so much that they did that. "Your mother means well, but she has a kind heart and truly wants to see the good in everyone. Good, that we both know doesn't always exist. If this girl is threatening your family there, then you do whatever it takes to protect them. Ignore the haters and rise above. Be strong, son."

I rolled my eyes. I loved my parents, I really did. They were like night and day, but in a way that just meant they complimented each other well, opposites attract and all that nonsense. I could already hear them bickering about my dilemma in the background.

"It's late. I'll talk to you both later. I'm going to bed now," I said, hanging up before they even responded.

Coyotes shifters mated for life, but the family unit or pack mentality of our brothers, the wolves, was not ingrained in us. Most parents kicked their kids to the curb the second they reached adulthood, and while they maintained alliances, the family unit generally consisted of just the mated pair after child rearing. Whereas our animal counterparts may have half a dozen whelp in one litter, shifters only had one or at most two whelp, more like our human sides.

By nature, wolves and coyotes are natural enemies, but our humanity allows us to live amicably. There have been instances in the history of the doghouse of dominance issues amongst the different canine breeds. My kind was by far the most adaptable and as Alpha of the doghouse, I've never personally had any issues.

I knew others of my kind did though. While we were adaptable, we also had the tendency to be conniving. My mother believed in killing others with kindness and rising above these stereotypes despite their validity. My father on the other hand, was a great manipulator who weaseled his way through life using whatever means necessary. I was more like my mother, but I couldn't deny there was a bit of my father in me, too.

It took some time for me to fall asleep as I thought through everything. There was so much on my mind and I didn't know how to fix any of it.

Morning came too quickly. I was much like a character from the *Walking Dead* as I forced myself through each class. I desperately needed a nap, but there was always something or someone that took priority.

By dinnertime I was running on pure adrenaline and lots of coffee. I wasn't in the habit of drinking a lot of caffeine, so it made me jittery, but there was no other way to survive the day.

I had a couple of hours between my last class and my seven o'clock meeting with the presidents of each house. It was just long enough to grab a quick dinner and hide out in the library to finish my homework for the day. At least with that out of the way, I would hopefully manage to go to bed early tonight.

Chad and his mate, Ember, were making out in the basement of the library when I arrived. It was a section few people used, which had always worked out in my favor.

"Seriously? What the hell are you two doing here?" I asked, slamming my books down on a table and taking a seat.

Ember nearly jumped out of her skin as she quickly smoothed down her shirt.

"Brett? What are you doing here?" she asked breathlessly.

Chad groaned. "Go away."

I snorted. "Not happening. I don't have a lot of time today and need to get this project done. Sorry. Besides. You guys have a room to yourself. Go home and use it."

Ember blushed and twirled her hair in front of her face to hide.

Chad sat up and glared at me over the couch, but a big grin spread across his face.

"This is where Ember and I first met," he said.

I nodded. I'd heard the stories, though didn't know this was the exact section that nightmare had occurred.

"The way you told it, I'm surprised you ever came back here," I teased.

Chad just shrugged it off. "It was a rough start, but it all worked out in the end. We're just giving this place some more positive mojo."

I laughed. "Is that what you call that?"

Chad laughed as Ember smacked him and shot him a look that said he'd better not answer that. They packed up their things and said goodbye a short time later and I was finally alone to finish my project and catch up on all my homework. I didn't like having stuff like that hanging over my head. To me it was just unnecessary added stress.

At six-thirty I packed things up and headed to the student center where I had booked a room to host the meeting for the night. I wasn't looking forward to it, but it was necessary. I needed everyone in agreement if we were going to fight the accusations Jade Michaels was spouting our way.

I arrived first and purposefully didn't plan food. They always had water and coffee set up in the back of the room when booking for meetings. I didn't want this to drag into social time. That was the thing with the fraternities and sororities at the ARC; every event, business or not, turned into a social gathering that evolved into a party. I wasn't in the mood for any of that, which was why I didn't hold it at the doghouse and didn't provide food of any sort.

Ayanna was the first to arrive, but the others soon trickled in behind her. She represented the Panther House. There were only seven houses on Greek Row and the Panther House was the only one that didn't use Greek letters to represent. They were also the most elitist of all the houses, a sorority of nothing but black panthers.

Ayanna was a pain in the ass to most people, but for some strange reason she often put her bitch side on hold for me, and we were able to work well together. I had been nominated for Greek Row president after she had announced interest in the position. None of the other presidents would stand for it.

Each house catered to a different group of students on campus. Delta Omega Gamma, or the doghouse as we were often referred to was mostly a canine shifter fraternity. We didn't hold exclusive to that though. I mean, Chad was a damn squirrel shifter, and my sophomore year we had lost my good friend Matt in a battle. He had been a jaguar shifter. No one could really accuse the D.O.G.s of not being inclusive.

The Theta house that Kaitlyn belonged to was a mixed shifter sorority. The girls there had common interests, usually in guys and partying, instead of common animal spirits. Tiffany had recently won the nomination for president of Theta and was the only new person attending the meeting.

Roland represented Kappa Mu, a primates only fraternity. While the majority of members were of the larger species, like gorillas, they accepted all primates. To the best of my knowledge no one outside of the primate community had ever asked to join, so I wasn't sure how inclusive they would be if pressed.

Nu Omega was about as inclusive as it got. Led by their president, Zeke, their only requirement was no Alphas allowed. They truly held to the Omega concept amongst shifters. They were a loud, rowdy but fun fraternity and quite the jokesters. They enjoyed pranking the other houses regularly.

Lambda Beta Pi was perhaps the most interesting of all the houses. While technically considered a fraternity, they were co-ed. All their members carried the spirit of farm animals. They were a peaceful group and often rallied behind the ethical treatment of animals with organized protests and sit-ins. Their president, Jerry, had taken over mid-year of the previous semester when their former leader left to take a job offer with PETA.

And finally, Kimber led Chi Tau, another mixed sorority. They weren't the biggest party animals like Theta, just a bunch of girls who wanted a sisterhood. They didn't care about the type of animal spirit a woman was, they were all about girl power.

When all seven representatives arrived, I called the meeting into session.

"We have a lot to discuss tonight. Most of you have seen the flyers around campus. Jade Michaels is leading a crusade to take us down. That sounds dramatic and conspiratorial, but it's not. The administration has already called me in to discuss this. They seem to agree that this school is leading the way in inclusion and acceptance of all shifters and that Greek Row is an archaic system that directly goes against that."

Kimber raised her hand and I nodded in acknowledgment. "Chi Tau is all about inclusion. We're a sisterhood for those needing that acceptance. How does that go against the school's vision?"

"I agree with you, Kimber, and used your house as an example towards that. I have no doubt that Jade would reciprocate by pointing out the exclusion of men to your group," I said.

"But that's ridiculous," she argued.

I raised my hand to regain control of the room as the others began to murmur in disapproval. "I agree it's ridiculous, but I'm telling you this is what we're up against. Each house has it's on exclusionary policies. I have pushed back arguing that just because a sub-set of people choose to live together does not make us segregated or unaccepting of the rest of the student population. Aside from the occasional formal affair for brothers or sisters only, when was the last time any of you held a party that wasn't open to the public?"

"The Panther House still keeps lists," Tiffany retorted. There was no love between the two houses, and everyone knew it.

"Oh please," Ayanna started, rolling her eyes. "So what? At least if someone shows up on the list or with a friend on the list even, we let them in. Theta may not keep a list anymore, but they make no qualms about rejecting people at the door, even other Greeks."

Others began voicing their opinions too and I placed my fingers in my mouth and let out a loud whistle that instantly grabbed their attention.

"Enough. If we can't manage to get through one meeting without fighting, we're going to crumble. I, for one, don't want to see my house broken up. That's my family, and I know each of you feel the same about yours. We have to stand united on this or Jade Michaels, with the backing of the current administration here, could destroy all our houses. Is that what you want?"

"Seems a little dramatic to me," Roland said. "No one's taking down Greek Row; it's an icon to this school."

"And an outdated one in times of change," I said. "That's what's being pressed upon me."

"What are we supposed to do?" Tiffany asked.

"For starters, stop rejecting people at the door," I told Tiffany. "And throw away that stupid list," I said for Ayanna's benefit. "I propose we throw a Saturday party, all inclusive, opening all seven houses and inviting the student population. We'll keep it outside as much as possible, just one big block party on Greek Row to show Jade and the others that we're united in this, because they think we're not. They think we'll crumble under pressure and turn on each other."

"A united front," Zeke said. "I like it, the Omegas are in."

"Hell yeah, Kappa Mu's always up for a party and this sounds epic!" Roland added.

"Okay, Chi Tau will help with decorations and food."

Jerry nodded. "Lambda Beta Pi will support this. Just let us know what you need us to do."

All eyes turned to Ayanna and Tiffany. Both ladies had their arms defiantly crossed over their chests and were glaring at each other.

"Fine," Tiffany conceded first.

"Fine," Ayanna shockingly agreed.

"Okay, great. Calendars out. We need to set a date, get the word out, and divide up responsibilities between the houses," I said.

Ayanna stepped up first. It was no surprise really. The Panthers loved to throw a party and she was obsessively organized. It wasn't all smooth going, but only took a little over an hour to plan and for everyone to agree. With specific jobs in hand, and a date set for two weeks out, I dismissed the meeting and finally headed home.

My brothers were all waiting in the common room when I arrived. They knew how stressed I'd been over the meeting and were there to support me. This was what it meant to be in a fraternity, and why I would fight tooth and nail to keep us together.

I filled them in as quickly as possible on all that had been decided, then said good night. Exhausted, I crashed the second my head hit the pillow without even changing my clothes.

Jade

Chapter 5

"Two weeks? They're throwing a unified Greek party for the entire school in just two weekends?" I asked, still in shock at how quickly they'd pulled it together. I paced the floor of my dorm room as Kaitlyn, Melissa, and Violet stared at me. "Brett Evans is far better than I gave him credit for. I won't underestimate him again."

"Isn't this what you wanted though?" Melissa asked.

I snapped my head towards her. "No this isn't what I wanted. He's going to win. He's trying to show the administration they can be inclusive, when we all know they aren't. It's just a smokescreen covering the obvious problems their segregation causes."

"I think you're overreacting some," Violet said. "This party is going to be epic."

"This party is going to overshadow our bonfire this weekend," I complained.

"It won't," Kaitlyn said. "We got our information out first and a lot of people are coming out for it. Your concerns with Greek Row are valid, Jade, but there's still room for compromise. We don't have to destroy them to get what we want."

"Yes, we do," I argued. "There can't be both."

"Maybe there can be and this party they're throwing is like them extending an olive branch towards that," Kaitlyn added.

"I don't want an olive branch, Kaitlyn. I want to see Brett Evans waving the white flag of defeat!"

I didn't understand why they couldn't see my side. All three of them wanted compromise, but I wanted all or nothing. This was war. Those dogs had humiliated me and countless others. They had to be held accountable for that.

I could see that Kaitlyn was close friends with my enemies. I didn't fully understand it all, but I knew she was friends with the doghouse, and not just Damon. It didn't help that I'd seen with my own eyes how much Damon had changed. He wasn't the complete prick I'd known freshman year, but that still didn't justify what he'd done, what he was still capable of doing to others. It had to stop.

"Breathe, Jade. You're so stressed out over this. Change is good, but it does come with compromise. Did you really think we'd just take down Greek Row and they'd never exist again?" Melissa asked. I hated that she was often my voice of reason.

"No," I sighed.

"Can I ask why you're so passionate about this? I mean what happened?" Violet asked. She sounded concerned, and I knew I'd blown up a little too much over these turn of events.

I sank down into my loveseat next to Kaitlyn. I didn't want to tell them, but they deserved to know. They had followed my lead blindly until now and I owed them this.

"I came to the ARC looking for a second chance. Growing up as a coyote shifter had not been easy, even in the human world, but I'd tried to rise above the stereotypes of my kind. My mother embraces it all. She prides herself on being manipulative and conniving, though she's a free spirit, the artistic type always painting and gardening, we couldn't just survive on that, so she used her "coyote skills" as she calls it to get us by. I didn't want to be like her. I thought if I looked the part and smiled a lot, if I just blended in with the others that they'd like me, and I'd fit in."

"But that didn't happen?" Violet asked.

I shook my head sadly. "I went to a human school. They didn't even know about my kind, but the other girls called me a bitch and said I was conniving and manipulative, the mean girl in school. It was then that I realized that's just who I am. I mean, aren't all coyote shifters just like me? It's who we are and there's nothing we can do about it. I honestly thought that coming to Archibald Reynolds would be a chance at a new start. You know, a place where I'd be accepted for me, just as I am. I got my first tattoo and all my piercings the summer before freshman year. I'd finally accepted who I was and decided anyone else who didn't like it could be damned. Then I met Damon Rossi."

"What?!?!" Kaitlyn screeched.

I smiled and nodded, then rolled my eyes. "Yup, freshman year. And I really, honestly thought he liked me, for me. He said all the right things and made me feel good about myself for the first time. He asked me to a private party at his fraternity."

"No, no, no, no, no," Kaitlyn cried as if she already knew what I was going to say.

I gave her a sad smirk and nodded again. "Yup, I was his dog in the dog show that year. He played me and it felt awful. To this day I'm still not sure I've really gotten over it. Year after year I've watched them do this to other girls. I've even tried to intervene and stop it, but nothing seemed to make a difference. It has to end. They think they're superior to the rest of us, but they're not."

Kaitlyn launched at me, throwing her arms around me. "I'm so sorry! Damon was an enormous asshole and you didn't deserve to be treated like that. He's not that guy anymore, but that doesn't justify or excuse what he did."

"Don't you see, Kaitlyn, it's not just him. It's all of them, and not even just the doghouse. Kappa Mu is just as bad, and let's not forget about the sororities. The Panthers and Theta are the absolute worse. It has to stop."

Kaitlyn cringed. I should have called her out on it, but I just felt too vulnerable in that moment. I didn't like sharing this story with them, but they needed to understand that yes, it was personal for me, but also important for the school. I truly believed that.

"Okay, well, now that we understand better where you're coming from, where do we start?" Violet asked.

We got down to planning, agreeing to forget all about the Greek's plan and just concentrate on the bonfire rally we were throwing this weekend. It was my entire obsession for the remainder of the week. I dreamt about it and couldn't wait for Friday night to arrive. The campus was buzzing with excitement. . . okay, more so because it was a big event that hadn't happened at the ARC in several years, more than my rally and cause, but whatever it took to get them out there, I just needed them to hear me out so that they would understand where I was coming from.

When Friday finally arrived, I was a nervous wreck.

"Relax Jade. You're making me nervous," Kaitlyn said. She had come over to help me get ready. "We have the DJ, the food trucks, the wood is stacked and ready for the bonfire. Girl, we got this."

"Thanks, Kaitlyn. I couldn't have pulled this off without you.

I carefully did my makeup, got dressed, deciding on black skinny jeans and a black t-shirt with my combat boots, and I was finally ready to go.

"Okay, let's do this."

As we walked across the campus to the main quad where we had arranged to host the party, people were already gathering everywhere. The DJ was setting up his equipment and I checked in briefly with him ensuring we were on schedule.

Kaitlyn left me when she saw her favorite taco truck lined up, and then returned with two extra tacos.

"You have to eat, Jade. We don't need you passing out on stage as you get this party started."

"I'm too nervous to eat," I admitted.

"You? Nervous? That's not something I ever thought I'd hear," Kaitlyn teased.

Begrudgingly, and so I wouldn't say anything further to ruin my reputation, I snagged a taco from her and shoved it into my mouth. The flavors mingled like a party in my mouth and I moaned in delight.

Kaitlyn laughed. "Your love of food is attracting all the guys nearby."

I snorted and swallowed hard. "As if. They aren't looking at me. They're looking at you."

It was true that Kaitlyn was gorgeous, the sort of beauty that shined from within. She could throw on a burlap sack, put her hair in a ponytail, and go without makeup and the guys would still follow her around. I honestly didn't envy her that.

It wasn't that I didn't want a boyfriend, I'd just never been the kind of girl that attracted guys. A friend once told me it was because I intimidated them. My mother always told me not to concern myself for boys and just wait for my true mate, as she wished she had done. That was easier said than done when all your friends had dates on a Friday night while you stayed home.

After my pathetic track record with guys, I also had trouble believing that there really was this magical perfect man out there just waiting to cross paths with me and somehow that would change everything. Sounded like nothing more than a fairytale to me.

As more and more people arrived, the excitement in the air buzzed. I touched base with the DJ to make sure we were on track seconds before he fired up the music and cheers went up all around us. We decided to give it one hour before I would give my speech and light the fire, but he would keep the hype going and fun in the meantime.

I couldn't believe we booked this DJ. He always played at the biggest clubs and most popular fraternities in the area. Kaitlyn said she had a connection and once again she'd pulled through for me.

I danced my way through the crowd towards the stage passing through a group of Thetas. They were the worst girls on campus and always thought themselves better than everyone else. Aside from the Panthers, they were probably the most elitist group we had.

"Well, if it isn't the antichrist walking amongst us," Tiffany said. I was well aware of the Theta president and knew that none of the Greeks were going to be happy about my stance. I was honestly shocked to see they even made an appearance.

"Shouldn't you be locked in your house having your own little party tonight, Tiffany?" I said snidely.

"Look who's excluding who now," she pointed out, and I hated that she was right.

"Sorry. That was in bad taste and I don't really want to stoop to your level. Of course you're all welcome here. Enjoy the party," I said as I pushed through.

Kaitlyn was just up ahead, and I couldn't get to her fast enough. I hated everything the Theta girls stood for.

"Kaitlyn, don't forget the party next week is required for all Thetas. That includes you," Tiffany yelled over the crowd as the other girls giggled.

I stopped in my tracks and stared at my friend. What were they talking about? Kaitlyn couldn't possibly be one of them.

"Oops, was that supposed to be a secret?" Tiffany asked smugly as Kaitlyn glared at her. Even over the loud music I could hear her low warning growl and I knew at that moment it was true.

Kaitlyn had lied to me all this time. Maybe she was even trying to sabotage my mission.. I'd get to the bottom of things later. What I wouldn't allow was for these girls to think they'd just gotten the best of me. I whipped around to face them again.

"You really think I didn't know?" I asked and then laughed. It sounded a little maniacal even to my own ears. "Keep your enemies close, right?"

I tore my gaze from Tiffany and stared at Kaitlyn. Guilt was written all over her. It was like a knife being jabbed into my chest. I fought to control my breathing as my world closed in around me.

I had honestly thought Kaitlyn was my friend, probably the only real friend I'd ever had, and it turned out it was all a lie.

"Let me explain," Kaitlyn said.

"No need," I stopped her. "I get it. They needed insider information to keep tabs on me. I'm not really surprised you know, just disappointed it was you."

The tears streaming down Kaitlyn's cheeks hurt me to see, but I couldn't let her know that, so I lifted my chin and glared at her as I walked past her towards the stage.

The time passed in a blur as I kept my emotions tightly reigned in, refusing to show any signs of weakness. When the time came for me to take the stage, I realized Kaitlyn was supposed to light the fire. I was going to signal her, but now I didn't know what to do.

Melissa walked by me and I grabbed her by the arm.

"Kaitlyn was supposed to light the bonfire, but I'm not sure she will now. I think she's trying to ruin our event. Can you help?"

"Kaitlyn? No way. She's our friend," Melissa said.

"She's a Theta," I told her, and understanding hit her hard. She nodded. "Okay. I'm on it."

Feeling a little better about the situation, I slowly walked up the stairs of the makeshift stage we had secured.

I tapped the microphone to make sure it was on. A screeching noise sounded, and the music stopped abruptly as all eyes turned towards me. I gave an awkward wave and cleared my throat.

"Good evening fellow Warriors. Our founder, Archibald Reynolds had a dream of shifters of every kind coming together as equals. This campus doesn't always feel that way as we have groups that segregate themselves like the sororities and fraternities on Greek Row." I paused to see how they would react, but no one did. I looked down at my notes and was struck by conviction at the negativity in my words. That wasn't who I was. I crumbled up my speech and tossed it aside. "Tonight's not about that. Tonight is about inclusion. It's about everyone feeling accepted and welcome here. Everyone," I said staring out at Kaitlyn who I was surprised to see in position to light the fire with Melissa standing next to her. "That includes the Theta sisters that came out tonight. Tiffany and all you ladies, thank you," I said catching her eye just in time to see daggers being shot my way. I smiled boldly at her. "And to any of the other clubs, fraternities, and sororities that came out tonight in support of our cause towards a more inclusive campus, just as Archibald Reynold's envisioned."

Much to my surprise the crowd went wild with cheers. I genuinely smiled and knew I had done the right thing. A tingling sensation ran up my spine and made me shiver. The hair on the back of my neck stood up but not in a negative way. My body warmed and I took in a deep breath to still my rapid heartbeat.

I was only vaguely aware of the guy walking the two steps up to stand on the platform beside me. When our eyes connected, the entire scene around us faded away. It was just me and him standing there gazing awkwardly into each other's eyes.

"Jade. Jade, snap out of it. You need to signal for the bonfire." Violet said. Her voice seemed far away but when she yanked on the hem of my jeans, reality finally broke through.

I looked out at my audience as they watched the strange encounter and I wondered just how long this guy had me under his spell. Was he a warlock or something? I expected unease to set in, but it never did, and when he reached for my microphone and our hands touched, I jumped back from the shock.

He looked just as shaken as I felt, but his words were steady as he spoke.

"Hey everyone. Hope you're all having a great time tonight. I just wanted to take a moment to say a few words. When accusations of the Greeks being exclusionary elitists against everything

Archibald Reynolds stood for started to surface, my kneejerk reaction was to deny it, but there's some truth there and it's hard to hear. I stand here before you all to say that we hear you and we're going to work to be more inclusive on Greek Row. If you haven't seen the flyers going around, check the school social calendar. Each and every person on campus is invited to join us next Saturday for an epic all inclusive party opening all seven Greek houses for the first time ever."

More squealing and cheers went up. The noise was nearly deafening.

"Jade," he said, handing me back the microphone.

A strange feeling rumbled through me hearing my name on his lips for the first time and it scared the shit out of me. I wanted to run as far away as possible, but everyone had calmed back down and they were staring at me, waiting to see what I would do.

I cleared my throat. "Enjoy the party. Kaitlyn?" I meant to say Melissa, but Kaitlyn rolled out with the ease and assurance of a trusted friend. She smiled boldly back at me as if all had suddenly been forgiven and lit the bonfire. The DJ fired the music back up and the party was in full swing again.

I wanted to be a part of it. I really did, but I was so shaken by the strange events that had occurred that I couldn't even wrap my mind around any of it. Instincts had me fleeing.

"Jade, wait?" a deep voice said.

Mate, a soft voice urged in my head and I swore the ground shifted beneath my feet as if a massive earthquake had just struck.

I slowly turned and really looked at him. My eyes widened in shock as realization hit me. "Brett-freaking-Evans?" I looked up to the night's sky. "You've got to be kidding me!"

Brett

Chapter 6

I watched as she turned and ran away from me. I grinned and considered giving chase. My coyote was practically demanding it.

Mine, Mate, he kept repeating in my head. I was in too much shock to really comprehend what that meant.

I had come here tonight expecting to be slandered by one Jade Michaels, but she'd surprised me by tossing aside her planned speech and talking from the heart. I wasn't sure how I knew that with such certainty, but I did.

Never having met Jade in person previously, I only had my own prejudices and assumptions to stand on. I was prepared to obliterate her and make her look like a fool before everyone. It didn't take long to realize my coyote would never stand for that because Jade Michaels, the girl I had laughed at and called terrible names, was my one true mate.

God must surely be sitting up in heaven laughing down at the two of us.

In what world did Jade and I make any sense? My coyote growled loudly in my head.

My instincts were to find her and sort this out. My inner beast liked that plan, but my human side won this internal battle as I headed for the nearest food truck serving alcohol and proceeded to drink myself into oblivion and forget all about the most mesmerizingly gorgeous green eyes I'd ever seen.

I don't remember much of the remainder of the night. Flashes of people, loud music, and the dancing fire. I think I may have started a mosh pit and did a little crowd surfing. I couldn't discern what was real and which parts I'd dreamed.

The next morning, I was relieved to find myself alone in my bed. At least I hadn't done anything entirely stupid. . .I hoped.

My mouth felt like sandpaper and tasted like an ashtray. Had I been smoking? I never touched cigarettes or weed.

I groaned when I tried to roll out of bed. I hurt everywhere.

My bedroom door creaked open and I grabbed my ears from the stabbing pain that little noise caused.

"What the hell happened?" I managed to ask.

"He's alive, I mean awake," Damon yelled down the hall causing my head to ring once again. "Probably wishing he wasn't."

Karis pushed through the door behind him and smacked Damon across the stomach. "Would you be quiet already. I'm sure he's got a headache."

She walked over with a bottle of aspirin and cup of water and handed them to me without another word.

"You look like shit," Damon said.

"Thanks, I feel like it too," I said as I sat up despite the throbbing in my head and quickly downed the aspirin. "What are you two even doing here?"

Damon had graduated last spring where Jackson and I chose to add a fifth year to our college careers, and even before that he and Karis had moved off campus. They lived in a cabin a few miles away owned by Chase Westin. Since Karis was only a sophomore, they planned to stay there until she graduated. Damon and Karis were future Alpha and Pack Mother of the Alaskan wolves.

"Man, I haven't seen you that wasted since your freshman year. I knew you had it in for that girl, but I'm not sure how crowd surfing naked was making your point."

"I did what?" I asked him, certain I heard him wrong.

Chad walked in with Ember by his side. He laughed. "Yeah, you heard that right. You were definitely the life of the party last night."

"How are you feeling, Brett?" Ember asked sweetly. "I can make you whatever you want when you feel like eating. Just let me know."

"I'm good for now, but thanks," I managed to say.

Ember unofficially lived with us. She and her Chad were our resident squirrel shifters. Chad transferred to the ARC a few years back, and since he had previously been a brother at Delta Omega Gamma in his last human college, they had automatically placed him with us. Boy was he in for a surprise to find out that D.O.G. was filled with actual dogs. Our forebrothers had chosen the fraternity because they found the play on words hysterical.

As a squirrel shifter you'd think Chad would have found himself very out of place, but instead he'd fit right in. Sometimes he liked to talk a little too much, but that was just Chad and we all loved him. In fact, I was grooming him to take over as president next year since I'd be graduating in the spring and he still had another year at the ARC, maybe longer if he applied to the new graduate program for his master's.

"So what happened last night, really?" I asked, grateful the pain meds were taking the edge off my headache already. "It's all a little fuzzy."

Karis laughed. "I'll bet it is. You drank to the point you actually passed out, Brett. We were all worried sick about you. Damon and I spent the night here to make sure you were okay. That wasn't like you at all."

"Yeah, you turned into a lot of fun and caused quite the scene at the bonfire," Damon added.

"We did manage to stop you from attempting to walk through the fire at least," Chad said.

I groaned.

Ember shrugged. "Flying tacos could become an ARC tradition though."

"What?" I couldn't even believe what they were saying. "You guys are just messing with me."

"Unfortunately for you, there are dozens of videos capturing all of your most eloquent moments posted all over the internet," Damon said.

I grabbed my phone before they could stop me to confirm their accusations. Sure enough, I was tagged in seventy-nine videos from the previous night.

"Don't worry. Chase is already working on getting them taken down," Chad said reassuringly.

"You called in Chase?"

"What better computer nerd do you know of to handle this situation?

"He works with graphics, not this," I reminded them.

"Well, with his connections at the Westin Foundation, he's making quick progress. There were one hundred and three up this morning."

I slinked back down into my bed and pulled the blanket over my head. This could not be happening.

"Thank him for me, then go away. My head is pounding. I'm fine. It was just a crazy night."

"That's what has us worried," Ember said. "That wasn't fine, Brett. That wasn't like you at all. We're worried about you. If there's anything you need to talk about, we're all here for you."

"Ember's right," Chad agreed. "Whatever you need, buddy. We're all here."

"This isn't something any of you can help with," I mumbled under my breath, sitting up to face them again. No way was I about to admit that Jade Michaels, who I'd talked shit about and was ready to publicly ridicule, was my one true mate. Just thinking about it made me want to seek out another stiff drink.

I had to have misread the signals. Anyone else nearby could have been her. It simply couldn't be Jade.

Mine, my coyote argued in my head.

"I'm fine, really," I said, trying to get a hold of my emotions. "Please go away. I want to go back to sleep for a while."

"It's two in the afternoon. I think you should consider staying up," Damon said.

"In what life did you become the responsible one and voice of reason?" I grumbled.

Damon just laughed and pulled Karis into his arms. "You'll understand when you find your true mate," he said staring affectionately into his mate's eyes.

"I think I'm going to be sick," I said, covering up the longing I felt inside. My true mate. I knew now she was here on campus. Everyone knew us as archrivals. How could I ever let them know the truth? Jade Michaels?

I groaned and flopped back against my pillow.

Damon laughed. "Get over it. If you don't need anything, we're going to head out and grab a bite to eat. Want to join us?"

"No," I said. "But I will. Give me a few minutes to clean up. That aspirin is starting to kick in."

I knew from the videos that going out wasn't my smartest idea, but I wasn't one to shy away from hardship. I believed in facing things head on, except maybe facing my mate. I wasn't quite ready to deal with that bomb.

My plan was just to ignore the gossip, put a smile on my face as if everything was perfectly normal, and carry on with my life. I'd been at the ARC for over three years and had never once crossed paths with Jade. With any luck, I wouldn't ever again.

I could feel my coyote spirit mourning that thought. He clearly wanted our mate. I'd had an up-close view of mating with several of my brothers. Was I strong enough to resist the pull to her? I guess we'd find out soon enough.

Everyone was waiting in the common room for me by the time I finished my shower. Ten of my brothers stood there watching to see if I was going to do something crazy, plus five freshmen rushing this year. We hadn't even offered to let them pledge yet, but they looked as if they were already part of the brotherhood. I wasn't going to do anything weird. They didn't need to worry. I freaked out a little seeing Jade for the first time and had needed an escape. That was all last night had been about.

I most often hung out with Damon, Jackson, and Chad. Neal, Lachlan, Tyler, Brian, and Pete were there too. Even Sawyer and Reid were there, and they only stayed at the house on the weekends when we were hosting a party. Add the five freshman to the mix, Dylan, Asher, Finn, and the twins, Holden and Hudson, and we had most of the pack present. Karis and Ember completed my welcome committee, and I realized quickly they were all going to escort me to the cafeteria.

I shouldn't be surprised. We'd done the same to Damon when he was going through his mating and became violent. At that time Tyler was dating Karis. We didn't know what was happening, but that kid was lucky he survived their mating at all.

I wasn't violent though. At least, I was pretty sure I hadn't been. From the brief clips of videos I'd seen, I had been more like the life of the party. The flashbacks that kept haunting my memories confirmed that. I'd been stupid maybe, but not a danger to anyone.

My cell phone dinged, and I glanced down at it out of sheer habit.

CHASE: Dude, only for you do I work on the weekend. LOL Coast clear. Videos down.

I typed a quick reply.

ME: Thanks. I owe you.

CHASE: She's worth it you know.

ME: Who?

CHASE: Your one true mate.

ME: What?!?

CHASE: Only reason I know of that would make someone do something so out of character.

CHASE: I'm here if you need to talk about it.

"Shit," I said aloud. He knows. How could he know?

"Everything okay, bro?" Jackson asked.

Looking around the room I could clearly see how worried they all were about me. I'd never been on the receiving end of those looks. It sucked.

"Yeah, everything's fine. Just Chase giving me grief. All the videos are down now."

"Knew he'd come through," Damon said, lightening the mood just a little.

"I'm starving. Who's up for a late lunch?" I asked. I wasn't entirely surprised to find they were all coming with me.

We all headed to the cafeteria. It was all you can eat and the best place to feed this pack of dogs, and Chad. The guys surrounded me, shielding me from the aftermath of the wild and crazy night I'd had. I loved them for it.

Inside we separated to fill our plates, but Jackson and Damon never left my side.

"I don't need babysitters," I reminded them.

"Humor us for today. Anyone says a word about last night, I'll throat punch them. I don't go here anymore so they can't kick me out," Damon said.

"There's no need for violence," I insisted.

"A dingo can sneak in and destroy without anyone suspecting," Lachlan said, startling me as I hadn't heard him sneak up behind me.

"A dingo ate my baby?" Damon asked in a terrible Australian accent that had Lachlan growling at him. We all knew how much he hated that phrase. It was the fastest way to set him off.

"Not here, you guys," I threatened, allowing a little of my Alpha power to seep out. I wasn't exactly an Alpha, at least not in the coyote shifter world, but as president of the D.O.G.s I was their Alpha for all intents and purposes.

They were shoving each other and arguing still as I headed for the large table in the middle of the room that Chad had appropriated for us. I could hear people snickering and pointing my way. Perhaps coming alone and hiding in a booth out of the spotlight would have been a better choice, but too late now.

I hadn't always been a good guy. I did plenty of stupid things in my life at the ARC, but I had never fully been the horndog Damon or Chase had been. I'd had a few frequent hookups my first two years of college, but as I'd gotten older and seen my friends pair off with mates, that partying lifestyle had been less fun.

While I made my mandatory appearances around Greek Row each weekend, I never stayed long anymore. I'd rather be at home with my brothers just hanging out and playing video games with Jackson, not that he'd let me if he were playing for his league. I wasn't that good. But I still preferred to sit by and just cheer him on.

Coyotes carried bad enough reps without me adding to it by doing stupid things like what had happened last night. That wasn't me. I couldn't remember the last time I'd been blackout drunk, probably freshman year while pledging Delta Omega Gamma.

I stared around at my family. That's truly what they were. Coyotes may stick to smaller family units, but for me, I'd always have my pack of D.O.G.s too.

Just as I took a bite of my sandwich, her scent hit me. Jade was here.

Jade

Chapter 7

Kaitlyn woke me a little after noon, demanding to know where I'd run off to after my speech at the bonfire. I wasn't about to tell her what had happened. She was a wolf and I knew now she wasn't just tight with Damon Rossi because he was a wolf too, but she was super close to all the D.O.G.s.

I felt betrayed and it hurt like a bitch. That pain had tapered off by the reality that Brett Evans was my true mate.

Everyone said when I met my mate I'd just know. I understood what they meant. There was no mistaking the signals that had shot through my body at his scent, his voice, and especially his touch. Of all the people in this world, why did it have to be him?

It had freaked me out so badly that I'd fled. Apparently, he hadn't taken the news well either, because from the videos I'd seen floating around, he had gotten drunk and went wild. I knew enough about Brett to know that was out of character for him, which was why everyone on campus was abuzz about it.

When Kaitlyn showed up in my room apologizing and sounding genuinely sorry for everything, I'd given up on sleep and grabbed a quick shower without a single word to her. It was beyond rude and I knew it. A part of me hoped she'd take the hint and go away, but I was surprised how happy I was to find her still sitting there, waiting when I was dressed and ready to start the day.

"I'm not just going to disappear, Jade. I can't say I'm sorry enough times. I've tried to tell you, to explain everything. Yeah, I showed up to that first meeting to bring back information on your plans, and maybe even sabotage them if necessary, but I really heard you. I didn't stick around because of that. I really wanted us to be friends. I've had this guilt lingering over me knowing I wasn't being entirely honest with you, and I'm sorry."

"Why did you keep coming around then?"

"Because I like hanging out with you. Because you're the only girlfriend I've ever really had. Most of the wolves here on campus, at least those that are organized, are part of Delta Omega Gamma—all guys. It's really the reason Theta even offered me a pledge spot. I don't even like half of them. I'm the only one in our sorority house that has my own room. That was a deal I made with them when I agreed to pledge. They wanted my connections to the D.O.G.s, and I wasn't afraid to use that to my benefit."

"Why didn't you just tell me?"

She sighed and looked miserable. "You hate the Greeks so much. I was convinced if you knew the truth, you'd hate me, too. But I won't accept that. I've never actually lied to you or pretended to be anyone I'm not. I simply withheld the fact that I was a Theta sister."

"That's sort of a lie by omission."

"Maybe, but I have to try at least. I wasn't sure you would ever even speak to me again, but here we are," she said optimistically. "And, even though you sent Melissa to take over my job, you still called my name out to light that bonfire."

I rolled my eyes. "I was nervous, and it just came out like we practiced."

"You never get nervous, so that's bullshit. You trusted I'd be there despite knowing the truth about me. I'm holding on to that because our friendship is really important to me and I'm not just going to walk away from you because you're mad at me."

"Fine," I said. It was getting late in the afternoon and I was starving. It was normal for me to sleep in. Coyotes tended to be most active at night. I tried hard not to schedule any classes before eleven in the morning. "I'm hungry. You coming to lunch or not?"

Kaitlyn lit up and squealed a little. She threw her arms around me for a quick hug. "Wherever you want to go," she said.

I laughed and knew she was playing nice. Kaitlyn always knew what she wanted, especially when it came to food, and never bothered to ask anyone else's opinion on the subject.

"That's a first," I teased.

She rolled her eyes. "Just this once."

It was strange how normal and easy it felt to be with Kaitlyn after everything that had happened. I wanted to stay mad at her, but I found I couldn't. She was my best friend and I didn't want to let that go either, even knowing she was my sworn enemy.

Maybe that was a little dramatic. The entire showdown with Tiffany last night had shown me that I was being hypocritical to just blindly hate them all. I still hated what they stood for, but I guess I could understand the need to fit in too, maybe. I mean after all, I wanted inclusion, wasn't that seeking my own sort of acceptance?

That reality had hit me after talking with Tiffany. It was why I had trashed my speech and refused to talk bad about the Greeks. I had been certain that Brett Evans was going to trash me in slander when he got on that stage, but he hadn't. He'd pretty much supported my efforts. That, combined with the realization that he was my true mate, had shaken me to my very core.

"Jade? Where'd you go just then?" Kaitlyn asked, sounding a little concerned.

"Sorry, just lost in my own head," I said, trying to compose myself. "How about the cafeteria?"

"Sure, let's go," she said, ushering me out of my room.

Things felt normal as we walked across campus. Still Kaitlyn steered the conversation into neutral, light territory as if she were still walking on eggshells of uncertainty with me.

I knew the moment I stepped into the cafeteria that Brett was there. I didn't know how I knew it, I just did. I wanted to turn and walk back out, tell Kaitlyn I changed my mind, but I knew her too well and she'd drill me for answers.

I got a plate and piled on some food. I wasn't even sure what and I didn't care. My skin felt like it was dancing over my body, similar to that itch I feel when I really need to shift, or just before a really amazing orgasm.

It was driving me nuts, and I was more than a little irritated, but I pushed it down and refused to even look in the direction that I knew Brett was sitting.

Kaitlyn tried to go to the dining area the D.O.G.s were hanging out in, but I steered her away into another. I was not ready to face him. If he came after me, well, I'd cross that bridge if and when I came to it. In the meantime, until I could get a grasp on my emotions and figure out what the hell I was going to do, I needed to stay as far away from Brett Evans as possible.

"Are you okay, Jade? You just seem on edge today," Kaitlyn said. "Are you still mad at me?"

"No," I sighed. "I'm not really mad. I'm just dealing with some stuff."

"Like. . ."

I shook my head. "Like stuff I don't want to talk about."

She looked genuinely hurt and her bottom lip protruded.

"I'm serious. It's, um, personal."

"Who better to discuss personal stuff with than your best friend? At least I hope I'm your best friend, because you are mine." She watched me with hope and visibly relaxed when I smiled and nodded.

For one insane moment I considered confiding in her.

"Kaitlyn, girl, what are you doing hiding over there in the corner?" Damon Rossi yelled across the room.

I looked up just in time to see the majority of the doghouse walking our way. My eyes connected with Brett's as he hung back behind the others. He seemed as hesitant to approach me as I did him. A physical bolt of pain shot through my body, radiating from my heart. My coyote whined in my head as I recognized the signs of rejection.

I couldn't breathe. My heart was racing. I had to get out of there quickly.

"Looks like your friends have found you. I'm gonna just go," I said, leaving my tray and everything as I rose and practically ran to get out of there as fast as I could. I didn't even give Kaitlyn time to react to my abrupt exit.

I could feel Brett's eyes on me, but I didn't turn around. Normally I wasn't an overly emotional person, but the feelings invoked within from the mating call were too much to bear.

Deep down, I knew Brett wouldn't choose me. We were too different, and I certainly wasn't his type. He wasn't mine either, so I was fine with that, or so I had thought before I truly felt rejected just from the look on his face. How much worse would it be when he finally said the words?

I practically ran across campus to put as much space between us as possible. I was so distraught that I didn't even notice he was following me until he yelled out.

"Jade, would you just stop and wait up?"

I nearly toppled over in shock. Why was Brett following me? I came to a halt managing not to faceplant on the grass in the middle of the quad, and then slowly turned to face him. My arms crossed defensively still feeling the sting from a few moments ago.

"What do you want?" I asked, a little harsher than I meant for it to sound.

Murmurs began all around us and soon a small crowd began to form. They all had their phones up with cameras pointed at us. It was like they were just waiting for fireworks or something. Did they somehow know about us?

Panic started to set in at the mere thought. I didn't want anyone to know Brett was my true mate. I knew he was going to reject me, and I'd end up being a laughingstock from it all.

"What the hell are you guys doing?" he asked.

"I'm not about to miss the next big explosion, even if you will magically get them taken down," one guy admitted.

"What are you talking about?"

"Are you kidding?" someone else said. "The way you crashed Jade's event last night, you two are the biggest talk around campus. Everyone's waiting to see how she retaliates or who strikes next."

I groaned and I heard a low growl reverberate from Brett. At least he wasn't any happier about this than I was.

"I didn't crash the event," he insisted.

I'd seen the videos that morning and could understand where they were coming from. I had been so shocked by everything that'd I'd run back to my room with my tail between my legs just trying to process what had happened.

If there was such a thing as a mating bond, I was praying my thoughts would get through to him loud and clear. *Shut up and do not engage, it will only make things worse.*

"I didn't crash the goddamn event," he yelled a little louder.

I couldn't wait around for the outcome, so I turned, pushed through a few people behind me, and ran as fast as I could, the second I was able to break away. The worst part, my emotions got the best of me and I started to cry. I never cried. I didn't even know why I was crying.

Brett

Chapter 8

I thought watching her flee the dining room had been hard and I couldn't stop myself from going after her, but seeing tears stream down her face when she ran away the second time was nearly my undoing.

I just wanted to talk to her. I needed that, but I quickly realized this was not the time or place. I chose not to follow her again. Brushing off the inquiries from too many nosey people, I headed back to the doghouse.

Jackson was the only one home when I got there. He gave a half wave in my direction as he yelled at the television screen. I could tell by his intensity that he was sucked into a league match and I knew there was no point in asking him if I could join in. He was far too competitive for me, and I knew I wasn't going to be able to fully concentrate anyway. No sense in putting either of us through that frustration.

Instead, I locked myself in my room. I ran another search for the videos of the bonfire and there were none to be found. Chase was good. I owed him for this.

Next, I tried to drown myself in homework. After a few hours of rereading the same passage a dozen times, I gave up and laid down in bed with a book. That worked for a while. Usually I could immerse myself in a good book, but I never really reached that point.

Frustrated I finally gave up, set the book aside then got up, stripped to my boxers, and turned the light off. I put in my earbuds and cranked the music as loud as I could stand it. I wasn't sure how long I stared up at the ceiling before finally drifting off to sleep.

Music was still playing in my ears when I awoke the next morning and my head was still pounding. It was Sunday and I had nothing to do. I decided it would be best to just lie low and spend a quiet day at home with my brothers. So that's just what I did.

By Monday morning I was hoping for a good day where the craziness from the weekend had just disappeared. No such luck.

After the scene on the quad, I'd only managed to add fuel to the fire. Rumors were flying around everywhere, all of them false.

"Did you hear Brett yelled at Jade and made her cry? I saw a video of her fleeing the scene. He always seemed so nice, but that was low," a girl was whispering to her friend as I walked into my first class of the day. That turned out to be one of the nicer comments I heard.

The gist of it was that Jade and I were painted as campus enemies. There was talk about her retaliation plans at the Greek open party coming up. My favorite was how I'd sabotaged the bonfire and hadn't even had a single drop of alcohol, that it had all been staged just to make Jade look bad. My hangover headache going on three days still screamed otherwise.

The thing that surprised me the most was how protective I felt towards Jade through all of it. I didn't want her to hear these lies. Worse, I didn't want her to believe any of them. I didn't want her to think I was capable of sabotaging something she was obviously so passionate about.

Hypocrite, my inner voice laughed.

Fine, I had tried to circumvent the event altogether. I was capable of the rumors haunting me, maybe that was my problem. I had walked up on that stage Friday night with every intention of taking her down a few notches, of ending her plans to destroy my family and home, and to basically just make her look like a fool in front of the entire school. I would have to carry that guilt with me now, even though I hadn't been able to go through with it.

She'd given a nice speech, nothing like we'd been expecting. She wasn't the hypocrite, I was.

That moment when I felt her presence and her scent assaulted all my senses and I knew she was my one true mate, it had rocked my world and I had handled it in the worst way possible. Now I had to deal with the outcome and figure out what the hell I was going to do with my little emo vixen.

I headed to lunch alone choosing a booth in the back corner of the cafeteria. I let myself really think about Jade for the first time. At a glance she stood out as different, something I'd never been comfortable with. I cringed remembering how I'd called her a freak.

Every time I'd seen a picture of her she'd been dressed in all black, and her hair was a different color. One picture she had blue hair, another pink. At the bonfire it had been more of a dirty blonde. She had piercings and probably tattoos too, though I had not seen any. I normally hated tattoos because they made a person stand out and I was all about blending in, but I was intrigued and wanted to know if she had them or not. . .

In truth, I knew nothing about my mate. *My mate!* That thought equally thrilled and terrified me. I had a mate. She wasn't anything like I'd ever imagined.

Jackson and Lachlan slid in the booth next to me.

"I'd ask why you're hiding out back here, but I guess we all know the answer to that," Jackson said with a smirk. My heart skipped a beat thinking for a moment he somehow knew about me and Jade.

"Heard that bitch hates you and that she's plotting to disrupt the party this weekend. One source said since they keep saying fireworks are about to shoot off between the two of you, that she's actually going to be tossing firecrackers around. Okay, not going to lie, that sounds epic. Why didn't we think of it first?" Lachlan said.

I heard the growl before a tray slammed down next to mine on the table.

"If you guys are listening to those rumors, then you're bigger idiots than I thought. Jade's not like that. She's not out for revenge, or anything. She just wants this all to blow over. She's upset about it, and I don't like seeing my friend upset, so you better fix it," Kaitlyn said

"How the hell am I supposed to do that?" I asked, trying to keep the emotions out of my voice. I hated hearing that Jade was upset. It set off something primal inside of me, a fierce need to protect her, and it was even stronger now than when I'd seen her crying. I needed to punch something or someone, blow off some steam before I did or said something stupid.

"I think you should make a unified public announcement," Kaitlyn said, helping to keep me grounded in the moment. I fisted my hands, trying to steady them as my coyote surged to force a shift and go find Jade.

"I tried to talk to her on Saturday, Kait, and it was a nightmare which only made things worse." What I needed was a way to get her alone, somewhere no one would see or hear us. I had an idea. "Hey, can you do me a favor?" I asked, quickly pulling out a piece of paper and jotting down a note. I didn't even want to say the words aloud.

One downside to an all shifter college was that enough animals had accelerated hearing that there was always someone listening.

Kaitlyn took the note from me and read it. Her eyes widened, as a huge smile broke out across her face and she nodded. I grabbed her arm as she picked up her tray and started to walk away.

"Not a word to anyone. Not even these idiots," I said nodding towards Jackson and Lachlan.

She was still happily smiling when she nodded and left to sit across the room. I sighed when I saw Jade waiting there for her. I really hoped this plan didn't backfire. I needed to not only straighten out this mess I'd accidentally created, but I also needed time alone with my mate to find out just what it was that made her so special for me.

Jade

Chapter 9

Kaitlyn had been talking to Brett. Just seeing him across the dining room made my heart race. I was in big trouble. I didn't want to be attracted to him. He embodied everything I had once tried to be and now stood against, yet there was this part of me that wanted to reach out and know him better.

Kaitlyn didn't talk to him long. I saw him pass her a piece of paper and then she picked up her tray and walked over to join me instead.

"You could have sat with your friends," I told her.

"I am," she said. "And hi to you too. I see you're all sunshine and roses today."

I rolled my eyes. "Have you heard the latest rumors?"

She growled.

I laughed. "I'll take that as a yes."

"I know it's a touchy subject and I'm sure you're not entirely over me lying to you, but for the sake of only speaking the truth, Brett is one of my favorite people here on campus, and so are you, so I don't particularly enjoy hearing the gossip line flooded with lies about two of my favorite people. It sucks."

"Tell me about it. So you and Brett Evans are close?" I asked, trying not to growl at her. The hairs on the back of my neck were standing up and I didn't like the territorial feelings I got thinking of the two of them together.

Get a grip, Jade, I scolded myself.

Kaitlyn laughed. "Not in the way you're making it sound. There's never been a thing. Like ever! Eww! I mean he's a great guy, fun, always making people laugh, and he'd literally give the shirt off his back to help a friend, but he's more like the brother I never had. Besides, I'm still holding out for my true mate," she surprised me by saying. She sighed sadly. "I'm not sure he's ever going to find me. Feels like everyone around me is finding their true mates. Anyway, you're not interested in Brett, are you?"

I had just taken a drink and spat it all over the table.

Kaitlyn giggled. "Yeah, that's what I thought. Could make for some much juicier rumors though," she said grinning evilly.

I shook my head. "You wouldn't dare!"

She laughed. "No, I'd never do that. I know he's not exactly one of your favorite people, and he's not your biggest fan either."

Ouch! Her words stung more than I cared to admit.

Thankfully she didn't even notice and kept on talking. "And I know you aren't going to be super happy about this, but please Jade. For me?"

I didn't know what she was talking about, but she shifted her eyes around to make certain no one was watching us too closely, then she took out a piece of paper and slid it across.

"What's this?" I asked.

"Shhh," she hushed me, likely drawing more attention by her doing that and her creepiness than by my question.

I unfolded the paper and was hit by Brett's scent. I quickly read it.

Tonight at Midnight by the Lake. Please.

That's all it said. I turned it over to see if there was more and shrugged. I looked across the room and found Brett watching me closely. I gave him a slight nod before I could stop myself. His face relaxed into a beautiful swoon-worthy smile.

You cannot start crushing on him, I chastised myself.

"Now, rip it up or eat it or something to dispose of the evidence," Kaitlyn leaned in and whispered.

I snorted, folded it back up and shoved the note into my pocket. "I am not eating it."

She shrugged. "That's always what they do in the movies."

"My life is definitely not movie-worthy."

Kaitlyn laughed by didn't argue with me. We changed the subject and enjoyed the rest of our mealtime before parting ways for our afternoon classes.

When my final class was complete, I headed back to my dorm to just relax and overthink the whole Brett note in peace. Midnight seemed like a strange time to ask me to meet. Maybe he didn't want anyone to see us together. Why would that be? All sorts of negative situations flooded my brain.

I opened the door to my room feeling deflated.

"Finally, I didn't think you'd ever get back," Kaitlyn said, scaring me half to death.

I jumped and screamed. My first instinct was to fight, but once I realized it was Kaitlyn, I forced myself to calm down.

"Are you insane? What are you doing in my room? You scared the life out of me," I yelled.

"Sorry. Your RA let me in. She knows we're friends."

"I wasn't expecting you."

"I'm sorry. I didn't mean to scare you. There's just something you need to know."

My gut instinct put me on the defense wondering what was wrong.

"It's nothing bad. It's just that the note was vague on purpose. The lake is a pretty generic location to meet. Brett did that because he knew I knew where he meant and could tell you," she explained.

I was not about to tell her that I had already learned I had a built-in Brett detector and was positive I could find him without her instructions. To admit that would mean confessing far more than I was ready to.

"Okay, so go on," I said instead.

Kaitlyn gave me very specific coordinates to put into my phone and some instructions on how to find this obscure place on the cliff overlooking the river. I had an eerie feeling I knew the exact place.

"So, why midnight? Isn't that kind of late?" I asked her.

She shrugged. "Well, aren't you coyotes more nocturnal anyway?"

"Well yeah," I said. "It's not like I'd be sleeping at that time anyway. It just seemed like an odd thing for him to ask. I mean most people don't go out that late, especially during the week, that's all."

She gave me an odd look. "Jade, you do know he's a coyote shifter too, right?"

I felt like my eyes were going to bug out of my head. "He is? I mean, I knew there were a couple of us here, but I told you I'd never met anyone else. I guess I thought the doghouse was mostly wolves, and since he's their leader he was likely a wolf."

"Nope, coyote. He's just like you, so he's used to staying up late too. Probably didn't even consider it an odd hour. He just wanted a time and place that you likely wouldn't be bombarded by cameras again. That video of you running across the quad in tears, I saw it. Brett mentioned that he tried to talk to you that day, but it had ended poorly with a mob attacking you guys. Was that why you were upset?"

"I don't even know. It was just such an emotional day," I answered honestly.

"You told me once that you never cried, so I was worried but didn't know how to really bring it up because I didn't want to upset you more. I didn't think you'd be happy about everyone seeing you like that, so I had my friend Chase make the videos disappear."

"Is that how Brett got the ones of him at the bonfire down so quickly?" I asked.

"Oh yeah. The Westins have crazy connections. I don't even ask."

Of course I knew who the Westins were. Everybody did. That part made sense, but even hours after Kaitlyn had left, I still couldn't wrap my brain around one simple thing—Brett was a coyote too.

Brett

Chapter 10

I paced the forest floor waiting and fearing she wasn't going to come. I mean, why would she? I'd acted like an idiot every time I'd seen her. I'd passed her a freaking note through a friend like we were in middle school. I might as well have added an extra line: "Do you like me?" with little boxes next to "yes" and "no" for her to check, and then pass it back to me.

I was pathetic. The worst part was, I wanted her to like me. I had this bad hang up about wanting everyone to like me, and I'd done some pretty stupid things in my life to ensure everyone did. This time it was different though. I needed her to like me for me.

Kaitlyn probably told her I just wanted to talk about what had happened, maybe even apologize, and come up with a plan to show a unified front at the party this weekend.

In truth, none of that mattered to me. I'd found my true mate. That reality had slowly been sinking into my thick skull for days. So what? She wasn't exactly what I'd imagined. What had Chase once told me? His mother had always said that God never makes mistakes when matching true mates. Belief in that is why his family had graciously accepted a panther into a wolf pack.

I realized I didn't even know what sort of animal spirit Jade carried. If I were being honest with myself, I really hoped it wasn't a cat. I loved Jenna, but I didn't know how Chase did it. Cats and dogs didn't usually play well together. I thought through my short moments with Jade, and I was convinced she must be a cat then.

A shuffle of leaves nearby grabbed my attention, and I turned to see Jade standing there watching me. Only a cat could sneak up on someone that easily. I sighed. Time to get this started. For better or worse, this is my mate.

"Sorry. I didn't hear you. Did you have any problems finding the place?" I asked.

She shook her head. "I knew exactly where it was when Kaitlyn gave me the coordinates," she surprised me by confessing.

"You did? I didn't think many people ever ventured to this side of the lake."

She shrugged. "It's always been a favorite place for me to watch the sunrise."

I crinkled up my nose. "I guess you're a morning person then. Sorry about the late hour." I hadn't even considered that. I never went to sleep before midnight.

"It's fine. I'm not a morning person."

"But you said you liked to watch the sunrise," I challenged.

She grinned and it was a beautiful sight. Happiness radiated across her face. "The sunrise is usually a reminder that I've been up too long, and I need to head to bed if I'm going to survive the day."

I chuckled. "Oh, so you're okay with this hour?"

"It's fine." An awkward silence filled us. She was still standing at the edge of the woods and I shoved my hands in my pocket not knowing what to do or say. Jade finally filled the void. "Um, Kaitlyn told me you're a coyote shifter."

"Uh, yeah, that's right." I said nervously. My coyote and I got along well. I knew plenty of others whose animal got them in trouble because they were quite conniving creatures and often difficult to control. I'd never had many issues with mine though. That was until this week when he kept trying to surge and take over to seek out our mate.

With Jade here, he was finally content and calm now.

"Can I see him?" she asked sounding curious.

"Uh, sure," I said with no good reason to turn her request down.

I didn't turn my back to her or walk away as I stripped out of my clothes. I wasn't about to ruin them with a shift. To my surprise, Jade never looked away and it was clear on her face that she liked

64

what she saw. I even caught her scent of arousal when the wind blew my way.

I smirked as I stood before her entirely naked, and then shifted in a flash. Most people, even shifters, feared coyotes at first. We had a bad rap. Jade didn't even flinch as I watched her reaction closely. In fact, she stepped forward and circled me to get a better look. She stayed just far enough away not to spook us like she somehow knew the boundaries of a coyote. Not that she had to worry, my coyote was excited by our mate's attention.

"He's beautiful," she whispered to her herself.

As I stared at her in awe, my coyote took advantage of the situation to gain the upper hand. He charged her, rubbing his fur against her legs as she giggled into the silent night. Losing her balance, she fell down on her behind.

"Ow," she said.

My coyote went into full alert looking around for the threat and growling out to no one.

"That was you, you big dummy. You tripped me."

He dropped his head and whimpered for forgiveness.

"I'm fine."

That must have been close enough because next he lunged towards her once again and started licking her face all over.

Jade pushed back, still laughing. "Brett, cut it out."

That was enough to give me control back. I walked away from her and quickly shifted back.

"Sorry about that. He's been very curious and excited to meet you. I don't usually have control issues like that."

She shrugged. "It's fine. I'm sure it's only natural."

I dressed back into my clothes, things had already gotten awkward enough, yet I couldn't stop myself from turning to her and saying, "Your turn. I don't even have a clue what your animal spirit is."

"Me? I'm a. . ."

I cut her off. "Nope. Surprise me."

She got up off the ground and rolled her eyes at me before she deliberately undressed in front of me. I gulped, thankful I had dressed so at least it disguised my growing hard-on a little.

Holy shit! Jade had the most perfect body I'd ever seen hiding under all that black clothing. I had definitely not been prepared to see my mate naked. Seconds before I was about to go all Alpha on her and likely claim her right there in the woods, she shifted.

Nothing could have shocked me more than the petite coyote that now stood where Jade had just been. A coyote? It was so rare to cross paths with one outside my family that I'd never really given it consideration. I knew there were a few at the ARC, but unlike the wolves who purposefully sought each other out, our kind kept to ourselves.

"You're a coyote?" I asked.

She responded by nodding her head just before shifting back. Her arms crossed her chest in a stance of defiance.

"Why are you so surprised by that?" she asked.

I couldn't take my eyes off her and my mouth went dry as desire hit me like a baseball bat to the back of the head.

"Put your clothes back on," I said through gritted teeth.

She startled and looked hurt. All the confidence I'd seen moments earlier was gone and I knew she was about to run again. Sure enough, I watched as she gathered up her clothes and started to bolt, but I was ready this time and I easily intercepted and wrapped her in my arms.

She shuddered against me and I took a deep breathe full of her scent.

"I'm sorry. I didn't mean for that to sound so harsh. It's just, it's the bond I guess. I've never wanted anyone as badly as I want you right this second. I'm just trying to hold it together and seeing you naked isn't helping." It was probably the most honest thing I'd ever told anyone in my entire life.

She went still in my arms and took a step back. I hesitantly let her go.

"Wait, you want me? Me? But. . ." she started then shut her mouth. She quickly dressed. "Better?"

"Not much, now that I know what you're hiding under there," I murmured causing her to laugh. "Why does that surprise you so much? I mean you're my mate."

She sucked in a hard breath when I said the word. I knew she knew it already, but even for me, saying it aloud, hearing it for the first time was a shock to the ears.

"I know," she said defensively. "It's just, well, look at you, and look at me. We aren't exactly a good match."

I shrugged. "I don't know much about you, but I'd like to find out more. So far, I only know that you are stubborn and defensive."

"Hey," she interrupted but I kept going.

"Not done yet, passionate, and more vulnerable than you show people." I raised my hands to stop her from protesting. "You have the greenest eyes I've ever seen, and mouth-watering breasts. Plus, you're a coyote, just like me. I guess that makes us more similar than you think."

"Why? Do you have mouth-watering breasts too? I hadn't noticed. And did you seriously just compliment my boobs in that speech?" she was trying to look angry about it, but she was smiling, and her eyes were sparkling. I got the feeling she liked my Alpha side and wasn't about to admit it.

I shrugged. "You need another look?"

"What?" she asked, bursting out laughing. "You're insane."

I grinned. "Why do you cover those girls up? Seriously? I mean, no one would suspect all that, under this," I said, holding up the sleeve of her black cardigan. A vision of Jade in a lowcut V-neck skintight dress flashed through my mind, making my mouth water. Then in that same thought a group of guys surrounded her, because that's what would happen. I growled and she startled.

"What the hell?" she asked.

"Sorry, just picturing you in a tight curve-fitting dress, but then remembered all the guys that would be drooling over you and my coyote does not like that idea, so from now on you only get to dress like that for me. No one needs to know what you're packing under there but me. Mine," I growled and without even thinking, I acted.

One minute she was just out of reach, the next I had her in my arms as my lips crushed aggressively against hers. I wanted, no, I needed to taste her, to feel her. Her body was pressed tightly against me and I could feel her curves in all the right places. Then she stiffened in my arms and fought against my grasp. I let go immediately, surprised by the look on her face when I had been caught up in a moment of passion.

I felt the sting then heard the slap before I even knew what was happening. My head jerked to the right.

"You may be my mate, but you don't own me like some piece of property," she yelled before taking off through the woods.

I was in so much shock that it never even crossed my mind to go after her and make sure she was okay. I gathered my things realizing we'd accomplished nothing, and I stormed back home.

It was late and I didn't expect to find anyone up. I should have known better. Kaitlyn was there with Jackson, Damon, Chad, and Neal watching a movie.

"What happened?" Kaitlyn demanded the second I walked into the room.

"Nothing."

"Nothing? She didn't show?"

"He wouldn't be wearing her handprint on his face if she hadn't," Damon pointed out.

"What? She hit you? Why? That doesn't sound like Jade at all," Kaitlyn insisted.

"What did you do?" Chad asked like he already knew I was the biggest moron on the planet.

"I kissed her," I blurted out. "And she smacked me for it."

Jackson and Neal started laughing so hard that they had to hold their stomachs.

"You really kissed Jade? The emo girl you called a freak? Why the hell would you do that?" Jackson asked.

I'd had enough and was about to lose it. "Because she's my one true mate," I growled before stomping off to my room and slamming the door behind me.

Jade

Chapter 11

I ran all the way back to my dorm room. I was huffing and puffing, and my face was streaked with tears. Why did I smack him? Why did I run again? I felt like an idiot. I'd just been taken by surprise. It wasn't that I'd never been kissed before, but this was so different and all the emotions that came with it just confused me.

I preferred to just lock down emotions and pretend they didn't exist, but this mating stuff was no joke. It was really screwing with me.

Brett had been nice actually, sweet even, but that kiss had been so possessive I'd just reacted without thinking. Now I wasn't sure how I'd ever be able to face him again.

There was a soft knock at my door, but I chose to ignore it. I was in no shape for company. It sounded again, but I stifled my crying into my pillow. I heard a click and then looked up just as the dark room flooded with light from the hallway.

"What the hell?" I cried out.

"It's just me. I wanted to check and make sure you were okay," Kaitlyn said.

"But, what? How? Why do you have a key to my room?"

I saw her shrug just before the door closed behind her. "Your RA was tired of letting me in here, so I convinced her to just give me a spare key."

I shook my head. Only Kaitlyn could manage something like that.

"You're not mad, are you?"

"No, I'm not mad, but I'm not really fit for company right now either," I warned.

"I know, but I had to check on you anyway. Are you okay?"

"Of course," I said trying to hide the fact that I'd been crying. "Why wouldn't I be?"

"Oh, I don't know, maybe because your one true mate is sporting a very red handprint across the side of his face. He deserved it, I hope," she said trying to lighten the situation.

Panic rose like bile within me. "He told you?" I wasn't sure anything she'd ever said had shocked me more.

"He seemed just as upset about it as you do, to be honest. I just wanted to see how things went, so I waited at the doghouse and a few of the guys were up waiting with me. We were just watching a movie when Brett stormed in clearly upset. I demanded to know why, and someone teased him about the red mark on his cheek. He blurted out that he kissed you and you slapped him for it. When we pressed him for more details, he yelled 'because she's my one true mate' and locked himself in his room. So, I ran over to make sure you were alright. Are you?"

"No, definitely not," I admitted. "The thing is, I don't even know why I slapped him, Kaitlyn. I mean he's Brett Evans. We're complete opposites if there ever was such a thing. Why him? And then he gets near me and says nice things and he smells really good, and just screws with my head so badly. I wasn't exactly opposed to kissing him, he just took me by surprise, and I reacted before I could stop myself. It's probably for the best that we just get the rejection over with sooner rather than later." I sighed, trying not to start crying again at that thought. I was such a mess.

"Wait, you're rejecting him?" she asked, sounding upset at the thought.

"What? No. He's going to reject me."

"Jade, sweetie, a guy, especially a true mate, isn't going to kiss you if he's planning on rejecting you. Is that what you're worried about?"

I nodded, then shrugged. "I don't have a freaking clue!"

She smiled. "Fortunately for you, like I said earlier, I'm quite experienced in watching everyone else do this. I've learned a few things. Let's start from the top; when did you first know Brett was your mate?"

I grimaced. "During my speech at the bonfire when he walked on stage."

"What? That was the first moment?"

I nodded.

"Girl, no wonder you ran, and he drank himself sick. I'm so sorry. You both already had prejudices against each other. That's an awful start to any relationship. Well, I guess that explains why he's been so weird lately and why you've been uncharacteristically emotional."

"Ya think?"

"It also explains why everyone on campus senses fireworks brewing between you two, only not the kind they are imagining."

I shoved my friend. "Kaitlyn," I said as sternly as I could muster.

She turned really serious for a moment. "I don't want you to break his heart, Jade. Brett's a really great guy, and if you are planning on just rejecting him, then I'm not going to help you."

"You really think that highly of him?"

"Yeah, I do, and I plan on asking him the same thing about you, right now," she said, grabbing her cell phone and dialing his number before I could stop her.

He didn't answer, so she hung up and called again. On the third try I heard him yell through the phone. "What Kaitlyn? What the hell do you want now?"

She stayed calm, completely unaffected but his aggressive tone. "One question. Are you planning to reject her?"

"What? What are you talking about?"

"Jade, Brett. She's one of the best people I know, and I don't want to see her hurt, so are you planning on breaking your bond with her?"

"Kaitlyn, I love you, but this is a personal issue between Jade and me. I'm not discussing it."

"Just answer the question if you actually want my help to get her to stop slapping you."

"I don't know her well enough to answer that question," he finally said, and I felt like I was going to throw up. "But I want to. I just feel like I blew it tonight, like really bad, Kait. I've never lost control over my coyote like that with anyone else before. I don't want to hurt her, so maybe it's best if I just leave her alone."

"Is that what you really want?" she asked as she reached over and squeezed my hand for comfort.

"Hell no that's not what I want. If she hadn't slapped me tonight I'd probably have already sealed our bond. Dammit, I'm a fool. I acted rashly and I moved too quickly. I deserved it. I'll be lucky if she ever talks to me again."

He sounded so sad that my heart melted a little towards him.

Kaitlyn squealed. "Okay, so there's a chance. Get your ass over here right now. It's time for your second chance. Don't screw it up this time. I'm texting you the address now. And put some clothes on. Unfortunately, I know you sleep naked the majority of the time, and she does not need to see all that yet."

I blushed furiously and her eyes widened. "Holy shit, you already saw him naked? Did you? No, you didn't, right?"

"Wait, she's there with you? Kaitlyn?"

"Oops," she said.

"Kaitlyn, is Jade there with you?" Brett asked.

"Yes, so why aren't you?" She hung up on him leaving that thought just hanging out there. Then she turned to me. "Details now!"

"It's not what you think. I just wanted to see his coyote for myself. So, he shifted for me."

She grinned. "But not before he stripped first."

"Yeah, something like that."

"But nothing happened?"

I shook my head. "No, he did try to kiss me, as you already know, and I did hit him for it."

"Reflex. He just caught you off guard. Or, was he really that bad of a kisser?"

I laughed. "I don't know. It happened so fast."

"You just need a take two. A do-over. Don't worry, I got you covered."

"Kaitlyn, what are you up to?" I demanded. "You know he's not really coming over here at almost 2am."

72

No sooner were those words out of my mouth, there was a knock on the door.

"Oh yes he is," she said with an evil grin.

My heart was already racing as she ran to open the door. She reached out and grabbed his arm pulling him into my room. I had to force control as my coyote demanded her punishment for touching our mate.

"She's not mad. It was just a reflex cause you moved too quickly and freaked her out. She couldn't even tell if you were any good at kissing, so really it wasn't even that. Second chance, my friend, don't screw it up. I suggest you pick up where you left off, just a little slower this time. I'm rooting for you both! I better get nothing but good reports in the morning," she said slyly before sneaking out of the room and closing the door behind her.

"She's insane," I said more to myself, but enough that it caused Brett to laugh and relax just a little. "I'm sorry about slapping you earlier. It was a kneejerk reaction."

He stared at me for a minute like he was trying to figure me out or something. "So you didn't mind me kissing you then?"

I shrugged. "I don't know, to be honest. I didn't wait around to decide. Kaitlyn says I should give it a second chance," I said and felt my cheeks heat. I wasn't usually the type of girl that blushed, but with Brett anywhere in my vicinity I was beginning to wonder if I knew myself at all. He made me react to everything in ways I didn't expect, mostly in highly emotional ways.

Brett stepped closer to me still looking unsure of himself. I was pretty sure Brett Evans was not the kind of man used to being uncertain about things. Everything about him screamed control.

His hand was shaking when he raised it to my cheek and rubbed gently with his thumb. It caused me to shiver and he nearly jerked his hand back until I smiled and nodded.

He took a deep breath. "Second chances," he whispered as he stared into my eyes before closing the gap between us.

My eyelids fluttered shut of their own accord and I sighed when his lips pressed against mine. This time they weren't possessive and impatient, but soft and gentle. He was hesitating. I leaned further into him and wrapped my arms around his waist.

That seemed to be all the encouragement he needed. His lips became more persistent, but still patient with me as he encouraged me to open up for him. As his tongue swept inside and swirled with mine, it stirred all sorts of wants and needs in me, but more so this sense of belonging that I'd never experienced before. I knew I could quickly become addicted to this.

His free hand snaked around my waist and kneaded the tense muscles on my lower back as he continued to kiss me senseless, and a soft moan escaped me. He smiled against my lips and started to withdraw. I wanted to beg him to just stay right there, kissing me forever.

He broke the kiss and smiled down at me rubbing soft circles on my cheek with the pad of his thumb. "Better?"

I scrunched up my face. "Jury's still out, you may have to try again."

He threw his head back and laughed. It was a deep carefree laugh that I instantly loved.

To my disappointment, he didn't rush to kiss me again.

"I'm glad Kaitlyn called and gave me this second chance."

I nodded. "She's pretty great, especially for a Greek," I said, rolling my eyes.

Brett laughed again. "You know, we've never actually met." He took a step back and offered me his hand. "Hi, I'm Brett Evans."

I snorted a little at his goofiness but played along by taking his hand and giving it a shake. "Jade Michaels. It's nice to meet you."

He grinned, stepping aside and offering me a seat on my sofa. It wasn't very big, and I sat on one side while he sat as far on the other side as possible. Things were still a little awkward between us, but I suspected that would be the case for a while.

Three hours later as he rubbed my feet stretched out across his lap and continued to pepper me with questions as we got to know each other, I realized I was very wrong with my first assumption.

It had only taken him a couple of questions to get me to relax. We'd been asking each other a mix of silly and serious questions back and forth for hours. I already felt more at ease and open and honest with Brett than I'd ever felt with any other person. It felt like a piece of me that had always been missing had just walked into my life in the form of this gorgeous, sweet, and goofy man.

Brett

Chapter 12

I wasn't even sure what time we had fallen asleep but waking up the next morning with Jade in my arms was the best feeling in the world.

We may look as opposite as possible, but when it came down to it, we had far more in common than I would have ever suspected. It wasn't just that she was also a coyote shifter, it was everything. We liked the same foods, the same games, and the same movies. While we picked different career paths, we were both looking to stay at the ARC for graduate school.

I could easily see a life together in our future. It was insane and quite surreal. It was shocking how fast everything was happening. All I could think about was that Chase's mom had been right all along. God really did know what he was doing.

I yawned and tried to stretch without waking Jade. I kissed the top of her head and she snuggled tighter into my chest. I chanced a look at my phone surprised it was already after ten. I needed to get home and change before my first class in an hour.

I lightly shook her. "Jade, wake up," I said quietly, trying not to startle her.

She groaned and stretched against me. There was no hiding how that made me feel. I grinned down at her.

"Keep that up and we aren't going to make it to any classes today," I warned her.

She looked up seeming a little confused as I watched the pieces start to fall back into place.

"Brett? You're still here? What time is it?"

"Around ten," I told her. "I guess we both fell asleep at some point while talking."

She jumped. "Shit!"

"What time was your first class?"

"Not until one."

"Then what is it?"

"People have been watching me constantly, you know, ever since the speech and the rumors started."

I clenched my teeth and tried to keep my calm. I did not like the idea of my mate being stalked by anyone other than me.

She rolled her eyes, seeming oblivious to the state of agitation that thought caused me.

"Don't tell me you haven't heard the gossip chain too. We're already being talked about by everyone on campus. Can you imagine if even one person sees you leaving my room?"

I started to relax, realizing the dilemma she was concerned about.

"My reputation's not that bad, Jade, and I'll set them straight."

"No, you won't," she squeaked.

"Huh?"

"We're not telling anyone," she insisted.

"Why not?" I asked, curious to hear her response.

"Simple, because first, no one will believe it. It's way too far-fetched. And second, just because you're my mate doesn't mean I'm backing down from my inclusion campaign. The bonfire last weekend still went really well despite my disappearing act and your party animal persona."

"You're seriously still trying to take down Greek Row?"

"Hell yes."

"Jade, that's my home, my family. I'm the freaking president of Greek society. I can't have my mate contradicting that."

"Well you're going to have to get used to it, cause I'm serious about this."

I was steaming. I already knew by her own admission how stubborn she could be. I needed to step back and think, then come up with a compromise that wouldn't be the end of the Greek system at the ARC.

"Make me a promise," I said.

"What?" she asked defensively.

"This isn't about your mission, this is about me. Promise me, Jade."

"I can't do that without knowing what I'm promising," she said matter-of-factly.

"Fair enough. I'm asking you to please keep a separation. Don't let the cause come between us, and I want you to actually come to Greek Row and spend some time getting to know the people there too, especially my brothers."

She scrunched up her nose. "No thanks, I've met enough of your brothers already," I said.

"You're talking about Damon?"

She gawked at me in obvious surprise. "He told you?"

"Yeah, he did. He stopped by the house one night all upset and said you and Kaitlyn came in for dinner and it took him awhile to figure out where he knew you from. He had brought you to a party as a prank freshman year," I said through gritted teeth. Knowing that Jade was my true mate made me want to go back and kick Damon's ass for it. "He said that he was afraid everything that's been happening was all his fault."

She looked embarrassed and wouldn't make eye contact, but I could she was still reeling over the experience.

"I put a stop to several of those stupid traditions. I don't know for sure if any of the other houses are doing stuff like that, but not under my roof. Besides, he lost, big time. He got razzed for weeks after that because everyone had said that even though at a first glance you may look a little different, you were by far the most beautiful girl there."

"No one said that," she said defensively.

"I swear to God they did. You can even ask Damon about it yourself."

She shook her head. "I don't want to see him, Brett. I don't want to be in that house ever again. You have no idea how humiliating that was for me."

I wrapped my arms around her and pulled her back against my chest.

"I'm sorry that happened to you. I don't have any excuse for it or valid reasons why any of us ever thought something like that was funny or okay. But people change. We all grow up eventually, even

Damon. Finding his mate changed everything for him. I think you'd really like Karis if you just give her a chance."

"I don't know Brett. For now, can't we just spend time together and leave the rest of them out of it?"

I sighed. That wasn't the answer I was hoping for. "Yeah, if that's what you need," I finally agreed.

"And I promise to try not to let the campaign come between us. I did hear you."

I smiled and kissed the top of her head. "Thank you."

"But now back to the bigger problem. How the hell are we going to get you out of here without everyone in this school finding out you stayed over last night?"

I really didn't give a shit who knew or who saw me with Jade, but it clearly meant something to her. "I'll be careful. I'm good at blending in. Whereas you, my mate, are definitely not."

"What is that supposed to mean?" she asked, getting defensive again. I had realized through the night that it was her security mechanism. Whenever she felt uncomfortable, she got snarky and defensive. I could work with that now that I understood.

"It just means that you were born to stand out."

She didn't have a comeback for once, so I took that as a win.

"Alright, let's do this. I need to get home, shower, and change before class in less than an hour."

She didn't move right away as she continued to lay against me. She took in a big breath and I knew she was capturing my scent, or so I thought. Instead she surprised me once again.

"Well, you don't smell completely terrible. You'll be fine if you don't get that shower."

I laughed taken by surprise. "Well, thanks, but I think you may be a little biased. What are you doing later?"

She ran through her to-do list for the day. I was exhausted just listening to it. I didn't think she ever really rested or stopped trying to save the world.

"Midnight then?" I asked sarcastically.

"Same place?"

I nodded. "Works for me."

"Okay," she said, hesitantly moving off of me. I got the feeling she didn't want me to leave any more than I wanted to go, but I also didn't think she'd agree to skip school and stay in her dorm room all night.

My phone dinged twice with incoming texts. I dug it out of my pocket to check.

KAITLYN – Not a single message from either of you?

KAITLYN – Are you dead or alive? We have bets.

I laughed and showed Jade, who groaned.

"I figured I'd hear from her soon. She knows better than to wake me before noon."

"Damn, how'd you manage that? This is probably the latest I've gotten to sleep in all semester."

"That sucks," was all she had to say.

I shook my head and stood. My legs were tingling, half asleep still from where she'd been laying on me. I wasn't going to complain one bit. I went to the bathroom, careful to check myself in the mirror. I knew she was worried about the possibility of someone seeing me leave, and I figured if they did, seeing me look like I was doing the walk of shame across campus would make things even worse than she was imagining.

Fortunately, it took little effort to look presentable. When I stepped out of the bathroom Jade was standing there watching me. She groaned with an irritated look on her face.

"God, that took you like a whole two minutes. It's not fair. No one should look that good after a sleepless night on my sofa." She pouted.

I took that as a compliment and gave her a cocky grin. "So, you think I look good?"

She rolled her eyes. "You know you do."

"You're kind of grumpy in the morning. Has anyone ever told you that before?"

"Yeah, I've heard it a time or two. You'll get used to my sunny disposition." She managed to say that with a straight face that cracked me up.

I leaned down and kissed her, morning breath and all.

"I'd ask you to meet me for lunch, but something tells me you'd say no, and I don't like hearing that word come from you." It was true, every time it felt like a massive bee sting.

"Kaitlyn already beat you to it anyway. I'm meeting her in an hour."

"She's a good friend."

She sighed. "I'm still not happy that she kept the truth from me, or that you, I might add, sent her in to spy on me. Backfired on you, because I've decided I'm not giving her back. She can secret spy and go all double agent on your ass."

"Fair enough."

We stood there for a while just staring at each other and not talking. It should have been awkward, but it wasn't.

"I really don't want to leave," I confessed.

"Too bad, because some of us can't look like perfect Ken dolls in under two minutes."

"What? I love this first look of the morning, Jade, all bushy hair and raccoon eyes."

Her eyes went wide. "What?" she shrieked and ran into the bathroom. "Why didn't you tell me I looked like I just walked out of a horror novel.

I looked at her like she had too heads. "Jade, don't you know you're beautiful no matter how you look?"

"That's what someone says to an ugly person, Brett."

"I'm not going to win this, am I?" I asked as I watched her scrub her face clean.

She patted it dry with a towel and looked up at me. It was the first time I'd seen her without any makeup at all. I sucked in a sharp breath debating my options once again. My alarm went off with my thirty-minute warning to get to class. I sighed in irritation. I had to go.

I stepped into the bathroom and took her face in both my hands. "So beautiful," I said, caressing her cheek. I gave her one final kiss I knew would linger for the both us throughout the day. "See you at midnight."

It took a lot to walk out of that room, but I did. I checked the hall, it was clear. I kept my head down and walked with purpose. No one noticed me. I made it back to the house, changed my shirt and grabbed my stuff before sprinting across campus just in time for class.

Jade

Chapter 13

At eleven o'clock on the dot, Kaitlyn called.

"I know Brett is in class and wouldn't miss it, so you are finally free to talk. I'm picking you up in five minutes, meet me behind your dorm. I want to hear all about it over lunch. Don't worry, we're having Jack's, off campus. My treat, no arguments."

"But I just got out of the shower," I argued. "I need more than five minutes to get ready."

"Jade, you don't need to impress me with your smoking hot looks, just get your ass in the car."

I huffed and hung up the phone. I set a timer for five minutes and got to work as fast as I could. I didn't have time for my normal full makeup regime, but I managed the bare minimum and at least looked somewhat presentable by the time the buzzer on my timer went off at the same time a horn honked outside.

I went to grab my bag and headed out. As I passed by my closet, I caught a glimpse of myself in the mirror that hung on the door. I was still wrapped in a towel. I came to a screeching halt.

The horn honked again.

"I'm going as fast as I can, Kaitlyn," I yelled out to my empty room, knowing she likely didn't hear me.

While wolf shifters especially had super hearing, most shifters had extraordinary hearing too, so all the dorms were built with added buffer between the walls. I couldn't be certain that Kaitlyn heard me.

Not wasting any time, I ran back into the bathroom and threw my towel over the shower curtain rod, then streaked back into my room to grab clothes and change before running out of the door.

Kaitlyn was still sitting there about to honk again and looking annoyed. I climbed into the passenger seat ready to apologize.

"I said five minutes."

"I was naked! I had to at least put on clothes. I told you I just got out of the shower."

"You took time for makeup?"

"I wasn't leaving without it, though I almost left in a towel because you were rushing me."

She started laughing and I knew all was forgiven.

To her defense, she waited until we were off campus to start questioning me. Like literally after we had just passed through the gates of the ARC when she started.

"What time did Brett leave this morning?"

I turned to look out of the window not wanting to answer her.

"Jade, what time?"

I sighed. "About 10:30, maybe a little later. We fell asleep talking."

"Just talking?"

"Yes."

"So, you didn't get your second chance kiss?"

I knew I was blushing. "Yes, but that was before we started talking."

"And?"

"And what?"

"Jesus, you're going to make this difficult. Wait here," she said. She parked the car illegally in front of Jack's and jumped out. She returned a few minutes later with a huge to go bag.

"What's all this?" I asked once she settled back into the driver's seat.

"Lunch, as promised."

"I thought you said we were eating at Jack's?"

"No, I said we were eating Jack's off campus so we could talk."

"That was pretty tricky. Are you certain you're not part coyote?"

She just laughed, then cranked up the radio and began singing along. I relaxed a little, even knowing the interrogation would continue later.

We weren't on the road long before she turned off onto a gravel road in the middle of the woods.

"Where are we?" I asked as a huge house came into view.

"Somewhere safe where we can talk. Plus, there are a couple of friends I'm dying to introduce you to," Kaitlyn said.

She put the car in park, turned off the ignition, and tossed the keys onto the dashboard. At least I had a means of escape if it came down to it. I looked around. It seemed okay, nice even. I hesitantly opened the door. The stench of wolf was everywhere.

"What is this place?"

"Come on, I'll explain inside," she said.

I didn't feel like I had any other choice but to follow her. The front door opened before we reached the front porch and two women stepped out.

"Here, let me grab that," the first one said. She had beautiful dreadlocks and looked quite exotic. I was certain I'd never seen her before. "Come on in."

She took the bags to the kitchen as we all followed. The other girl had dark hair and wore glasses too big for her face, yet it seemed to work for her. She looked super cute. There was something very familiar about her, but I couldn't quite put my finger on it.

"Hi," she finally said, like she couldn't hold back any longer. "I'm Ember. It's so nice to meet you." She took me by surprise when she hugged me.

"Hi," I said awkwardly. "I'm Jade."

"I know. I've heard so much about you, actually most of it from my friend Melissa," she said.

"Oh. Oh! Wait, are you Emmy Kenston?"

"I am, but all my close friends call me Ember."

"Yeah, Melissa mentioned something about you guys being friends." I thought back for a moment on what all she'd said and frowned. My hands went to my hips and I glared at Kaitlyn. *She wouldn't!* "Yeah, I believe she mentioned something about you mating one of the Delta Omega Gamma brothers."

"That's right, Chad," she said with a dreamy look in her eyes.

"You'd swear they were newly mated still," Kaitlyn said.

"Yeah, it's kind of disgusting actually," the other girl said.

"As if you're one to talk," Kaitlyn teased her.

The girl just shrugged as she started unloading containers from the bags we'd brought.

I rolled my eyes. "Let me guess, you're mated to a D.O.G. too?" I shot a dirty look at Kaitlyn before the girl could even confirm it. I was already certain of the answer.

She giggled. "Yeah, I'm Karis. I'm mated to Damon Rossi."

I was glad I hadn't started eating yet, because I think I'd probably have spit it out at her, or possibly died choking.

"What?" I sputtered.

She just laughed. "Yeah, after everything he told me, I'm not surprised by that reaction. Trust me I've heard it all. The biggest asshole of the ARC. The biggest horn dog of the ARC. On and on. Nothing surprises me anymore, but well, I just don't know him that way and never really have."

"I guess it's hard for me to see him that way," I muttered.

She gave me a sad look. "I'm sure. And I'm so sorry. Damon came home sick to his stomach that night you and Kaitlyn ate at the steakhouse. He feels terrible about what he did to you and feels like everything happening is all his fault."

"Is this some sort of weird intervention?" I asked Kaitlyn.

She laughed. "No. I've been wanting to introduce you to these guys for a while. I just thought that today seemed like an especially good day for it."

I rolled my eyes. "Because we're all mated to D.O.G.s? Is that supposed to be an insta-bond or something?"

"Wait, who are you mated to?" Ember asked.

"Brett," I said. "Isn't that what we're all here to talk about?"

Kaitlyn started laughing and Karis's eyes nearly bugged out of her head while Ember's jaw came close to hitting the floor.

"You didn't tell them?"

Kaitlyn was still laughing. There were tears in her eyes. "Nope. I didn't think you wanted to discuss it but figured you could use a girls' day."

I covered my face with my hands and shook my head.

"You and Brett?" Ember shrieked. "When? How?"

Karis started giggling so hard she had to sit down. "That's priceless!"

Kaitlyn came to my defense. "It's still really new you guys, but since it's now open discussion, dish the food, and then Jade can start talking."

I rolled my eyes. "There's really nothing to talk about. You already know everything."

"Um, this is the first we've heard about it," Ember said.

"Don't you live at the doghouse?" I asked her.

"Mostly, and I haven't heard anything about this. Must be the tightest kept secret ever."

"Wait," Kaitlyn said. "Chad knows. I came over last night and he stayed up with me waiting for Brett to get home from their midnight rendezvous that went south quickly. But Chad was definitely there when Brett dropped that bomb on all of us, so why don't you know this already?"

Ember frowned. "My mom had some big event she wanted me to attend last night. I just flew back in this morning and since he's in classes most of the day, I just came here to hang out with Karis instead. I already knew she had the day off. So, I haven't really seen or talked to him since yesterday evening."

"So Brett just blurted it out to you?" Karis asked.

"Yes! I'm not sure who was more shocked. I mean, I knew he was meeting Jade, but I thought it was just to discuss all the crap going on and to work on a truce." Kaitlyn continued to fill them in on everything that was happening.

"So. you met him last night and realized he was the one?" Karis asked.

I shook my head. "No. If all the videos hadn't been taken down of the bonfire, I could probably show you the exact moment that happened."

"Oh no. It was the pause after your speech, wasn't it? You just sort of froze at the end before you signaled to light the fire. You looked really spooked and then shook it off and finished speaking. It was longer than necessary for dramatic effect, and I'm certain that's when Brett walked onto stage behind you," Ember said.

I stared at her. "You're very observant."

"My mom's in a lot of movies. She's always pointing out the little details everyone overlooks. Habit I guess."

"That's right, your mom is Alicia Kenston," I said.

Ember smiled proudly. "Yeah, she is."

"That's so cool."

"Stalling," Kaitlyn accused. "So, we know what happened when you met Brett by the lake, but I am dying to know what happened with the second chance I gave you guys."

I rolled my eyes. "I already told you. We stayed up late talking and getting to know each other, then we fell asleep. This morning we fought, and he left."

"Wait, you're still fighting?" she asked.

I shrugged. "Sort of. He wants me to drop the inclusion campaign and get to know his brothers. Not happening."

Karis looked contemplative before speaking. "So, he's definitely your mate?"

I nodded. "Yeah, there's really no doubt about that."

"You're handling that way better than I did for the bond to be so new still," Ember said.

"Yeah, honestly, it's kind of scary how calm you are about it," Kaitlyn said. "Everyone else I know was freaking out by now."

"Oh, I'm freaking out plenty. I assure you," I said with a laugh, but was I? Not really. I felt like we didn't really have a choice in the matter. He was my mate, that was just a fact.

"Did he tell you, really tell you, how much the doghouse means to him?" Karis asked. "I mean he's been ranting about you non-stop since the start of the semester over this campaign of yours. He'd do just about anything to stop you and save Greek Row."

I wasn't sure where she was going with this, but I did not like the feeling of guilt setting in.

"That's right, but I've seen drastic changes in each of the guys as they've fallen to their true mates," Kaitlyn pointed out. "Brett definitely wouldn't be the first."

"True, but not on their principle foundation," Karis said. "Delta Omega Gamma means everything to Brett. I get he's a guy that dives in one hundred percent when he commits to something. You're not going to be any different there, Jade. I can see him easily accepting your bond, but no way would he turn his back on the boys."

"Not just the boys, but all of the houses," Ember added. "Did you know he was the youngest president in Delta Omega Gamma

ARC chapter history? He's been their leader since his sophomore year. That just doesn't happen. When Ayanna stepped up to be Greek president, everyone turned to Brett and begged him to intervene."

"He's as protective, if not more so, than any wolf I've ever met," Karis added. "He won't just abandon them, even for you, Jade. I don't want to see either of you hurt, so I'm just saying, pick your battles carefully. Being mated isn't always easy. It takes a lot of comprise. The two of you need to find a solution for this that you can both live with!"

I looked oddly at Karis. "You're very insightful for being so young."

She smiled. "My Oma says I'm a very old soul. Plus, being future Pack Mother of my Pack forced me to grow up a little quicker than most in some ways."

"You're an heir?" I asked, considering what that meant. I burst out laughing. "Damon Rossi is going to be an Alpha someday?"

Her smile brightened proudly. "A damn good one, too."

"But he's an idiot," I blurted out.

She just shrugged it off. "He has his moments. You just don't know him the way I do."

I thought about everything they were saying. If Damon could really change that much, would I too? If I were honest, I started this campaign out of vengeance, but I really did believe in it, too. Could I learn to compromise?

"What's your major?" Karis surprised me by asking.

"Pre-law," I said.

She smirked. "Then consider this your first lesson in many compromises. Find the common ground and start there. Nothing is worth coming between you and your mating bond."

Long after I'd said goodbye to my new friends, and thanked Kaitlyn for pushing me, or rather tricking me, into meeting them, Karis's words still lingered on my heart.

Brett

Chapter 14

Waiting until midnight to see Jade was harder than I'd expected. I craved her company, even her witty smartass comebacks. By evening my brothers were walking on eggshells around me. I was irritable and just wanted to pick up the phone and call her. The problem was that I didn't have her number.

All day I had to endure countless rumors being spread. Most were along the line of how much Jade hated me personally, or at least those were the ones my ears kept tuning in to. I knew it wasn't true, but it still hurt to hear them.

I needed my mate. I could just walk over to her room, but she was so adamant about no one seeing me leave this morning that I didn't think that would go over so well.

It was Tuesday already, and the open Row party this weekend would be coming up fast. There was a lot to do. I forced myself to go to the meeting with the heads of houses. It was my meeting after all. Everyone would have questioned it if I hadn't, but my heart and mind were elsewhere. I was surprised no one called me out on it.

Fortunately, things seemed to be running smoothly and I was happy to let Tiffany and Ayanna hash out the details. It was almost scary watching the two of them working together so well. Maybe Jade was onto something with this inclusion thing. If nothing else, for me it was eye opening seeing all seven houses working together without the usual drama and disputes.

By eleven I couldn't take it anymore. I left the house and went to the clearing on the cliff overlooking the lake. I wasn't expecting Jade for another hour but figured I could use a good run. I stripped and shifted, ready to dash into the woods.

A shift in wind alerted me to the fact I was not alone. My coyote turned and ran in the direction of the scent. It didn't take long for me to track Jade in the woods also out for a run.

I stopped and howled. She startled and turned towards me. Her tail was wagging, and I knew she was happy to see me too. Her coyote surprised me when she approached and rubbed against my fur. I was still in awe of the fact that we were the same species.

We ran and played through the forest. It was arguably the best time I'd ever had in my fur. As a coyote it wasn't always safe for me to shift. I did so often enough here at the ARC, but it was almost always under the protection of my pack.

The prejudice against coyotes held strong even in the shifter world. It was something only a few of my brothers could truly understand. Dingo's weren't much better, but here they were more exotic. Lachlan had confided in me that he faced many of the same preconceptions towards his kind back home in Australia.

The wolves though, they were strong and magnanimous. Even the humans respected them. They would never know the hardships my kind faced.

I worked hard to overcome such bias and stand as my own man, but it wasn't easy. My mother had mentioned something to that affect when I had spoken to her shortly after all the craziness began. She had wondered if that wasn't part of the driving force behind Jade. I didn't know at the time she was a coyote, so maybe there was some truth to that.

When we finally returned to the clearing, I shifted back to my human form. Jade seemed to hesitate a bit before following.

Nudity wasn't supposed to be a big deal amongst shifters. It was sort of par for the course unless you wanted to constantly buy new clothes. Every time I saw Jade naked it felt like a big deal though.

This time I took my time enjoying the view. What had I told her before? She had mouth-watering breasts. I licked my lips wanting a taste.

She crossed her arms over her chest to hide my view. I frowned.

"Are you fantasizing about my mouth-watering boobs again?" she teased.

I grinned. "Hell yes I am."

She shook her head and her cheeks darkened a little, but she didn't rush to redress. I knew she could see clearly the effect she was having on me. I didn't care in the least. She was my mate, of course I desired her.

I had brought a blanket to lay out on the ground. After doing so, I silently invited Jade to join me. The nights were getting cooler by the day despite an unusual heatwave so late in the season.

I didn't bother dressing, and I was thrilled when she followed my lead and joined me on the blanket without grabbing her clothes first. She laid back with her arms crossed pillowing her head. She was so natural and carefree, exposed and vulnerable. She looked beautiful in the moonlight and it took everything in my power not to cover her with my body and kiss her senseless.

Instead I laid down beside her and talked up to the sky.

"I didn't hear a peep from Kaitlyn today. I thought for sure she'd be all up in my grill with questions."

Jade groaned. "No, she left all that to me. I didn't even make it to class today. I met Karis and Ember though. They seemed nice."

I wasn't shocked to hear Kaitlyn had likely kidnapped her, but I was very surprised that she had already met my brothers' mates.

"I'm glad," I finally said, choosing not to make a big deal out of it.

"They said I should try to find some common ground on this whole inclusion campaign, that nothing was worth coming between mates. Do you believe that?"

I thought long and hard about that, staying quiet probably longer than I should have. I was still getting to know Jade, but there was a powerful pull I felt towards her. I hadn't yet been able to describe it or even understand it. I knew in my heart there was absolutely nothing I wouldn't do for her.

"A week ago, if someone had asked me if there was anything or anyone in this world that I would give up my brotherhood for, I'd have said, "hell no!" but now you're here, and I can no longer say that with absolution. My family and my fraternity mean the world to me, Jade. I hope to God I never have to choose between them and you."

She sighed. "I don't think I can ask you to do that, Brett," she said softly.

I rolled on my side to stare down at her. Fear creeped in. Was she going to break the bond and leave me?

"Stop looking so freaked out," she said, pushing me back down. "I just mean that I've really been giving some thought to that today. In no world do you and I make sense. It's comical even. You're like the poster boy for conformity and I'm anything but."

"Don't," I told her. "Don't say that. You are my mate. You're it for me. So what if we don't look like the perfect couple? We are the perfect couple, because you're perfect for me."

She rolled to face me. "That wasn't where I was going with this."

The look of confusion on my face set her into a fit of giggles. I loved that sound, like tinkling bells in the night. She tried hard not to make it a habit of smiling, but when she did, she was breathtaking. I couldn't resist the opportunity to push up and close the gap between us.

She sighed into my kiss and I struggled not to press her for more.

After a few minutes, she pushed me away. She had a dreamy look in her eyes which was probably the only thing curbing my disappointment.

"I was trying to make a point here," she said trying to look put off. But I knew better, and the smell of her arousal in the air only confirmed it and made me more confident.

"Okay, continue," I said, lying back and pulling her with me so she was tucked into my side and resting her head in the crook of my shoulder. That may have been a mistake on my part, as the feel of her naked breast firmly molded against me was making it a trial to concentrate.

She propped her elbow so her head could rest in her hand allowing her to look more closely at me. I just hoped she didn't look down. My lower parts apparently had a life of their own and nothing I could do or try to think of just then was going to dissolve the situation.

"What I was trying to say is that I get it. I understand now how important it all is to you. I don't really know why but hearing it from others made me realize that if we're going to work, I can't be selfish and only think about what I want. I may not care what anyone else here thinks, but I should care about your feelings."

"Really?" I asked, surprised it had come so easily. She was obviously open to a compromise and maybe even considering dropping it all? Okay, I probably shouldn't jump to that conclusion so quickly, but it was a start.

"Really," she said. For a moment she was quiet, and then she looked so vulnerable that I just wanted to protect her from everything. "I'm not really good at confiding in people, or trusting them, Brett, but I need to step back a little and have faith that you know what you're doing. I've already seen some of the positive changes you've made since taking over as president this year. I didn't want to admit that and it's still not easy to do so, now, but for the sake of whatever this is between us, I'm trying. I'm trying to push aside my own prejudices and anger, and trust that together we can still make a difference even if it's not exactly how I'd originally imagined."

I pulled her down to kiss her again, but only briefly.

"You're amazing. Do you realize that?" I wondered how much I should confess to her, but since she'd jumped, I was going to follow. "The open Row party this weekend. I was only doing it to throw it back in your face. I thought maybe by having a bigger, better party than your bonfire, would somehow show that we weren't changing or going anywhere."

She rolled her eyes. "I suspected as much."

"But, something weird happened along the way."

"Yeah, it's called mating," she snarked.

"No, smartass, I mean between the houses. We've always kept our segregation because it's not easy getting along, especially with other species. Most of us just wanted our safe space here at the ARC."

"I guess I never really thought of it that way before," she admitted.

"It's the truth. I'm not sure it's possible for me to lie to you. But anyway, that's not the point. For the first time since I've been here, all seven houses are at peace and working towards a common goal. Okay, that common goal is to take you down, but that's not the point either. The point is, that by opening up and being inclusive, instead of fighting more, we're actually all getting along. It's weird and I guess we have you to thank for that."

Jade laughed. "You're really bad at this. How did you even become president? I'm not really sure if I'm supposed to be proud of that or offended."

I could tell she was only teasing me.

"Maybe you should just shut me up next time," I said.

"Maybe I will," she said in a sexy voice just before she kissed me.

It was the first time Jade had taken the lead like that and my body responded quickly. I was already hard, but now it was almost painful. I wanted her so badly it literally hurt. As she swirled her tongue into my mouth, I relished in the feel of her tongue piercing. It wasn't something I'd ever thought I'd enjoy, but the feel of hard metal and her soft mouth played on my senses and heightened every moment with her.

I rolled us so she was on her back and I was towering above her. While we continued our kissing, my hand went to her waist and caressed the soft skin of her stomach as I slowly inched forward. She stopped me just before I reached her right breast.

Breathless, she pulled back and stared up at me. I gave her a cocky smirk.

"Too fast?" I asked.

She shook her head. "I don't know how to describe it. I've never been a very emotional person, but your actions seem to send that into hyper drive and it's just overwhelming at times. I'm just struggling to keep a grip on reality right now."

I knew what was happening, it was the same as when I kissed her, sense overload. Everything with Jade was just more heightened somehow. I understood what she meant. As I looked down at her I realized that just from our kissing and me touching her, not even in an intimate place was nearly her undoing. She was close to a release and holding back. Why? I didn't know and I didn't care.

I gave her no warning as I lowered my head to her closest nipple and sucked it into my mouth. She threw her head back and growled through gritted teeth. "Brett." There was no malice behind it, and I didn't let up.

It took no time at all and I didn't even have to head south to bring her to orgasm. She clawed at my back and groaned my name. I had never been with anyone so responsive before and it gave me a high I had never experienced.

Her body was blushed all over and she threw her arm over her face in embarrassment.

"What the hell just happened?" she whispered, and I knew she didn't really want me to answer that.

I kissed my way up her neck, moved her arm and found her lips. I pulled back with a sheepish grin. "That was awesome!"

"I don't even know how you managed that. It's so embarrassing."

She tried to cover her face again, but I wouldn't let her.

"Babe, you have nothing to be embarrassed about." I kissed her sweetly this time, so as not to encourage a round two. I was barely holding it together as it was, but tonight felt like I needed to focus on her and forget my own needs. I'd just handle that on my own later.

She gently shoved me away and I rolled over onto my back next to her.

"We aren't making much progress on the problem at hand."

"Oh, I think that was great progress."

She laughed and elbowed me in the side. "Brett," she warned.

"You have no idea how sexy you are. I'm just saying. If you want me to even attempt to keep my hands to myself, you probably should put some clothes on."

"And if I don't?"

I gulped and rolled back over to her. I could tell by the way her eyes were dancing that she was only teasing me. She looked relaxed and happy lying there next to me. It made my heart swell. I was an average sized guy, but she was tiny and vulnerable beside me.

"Careful what you wish for," I warned her.

"Okay, clothes and no more touching then."

I pouted. She didn't move to get dressed, instead she rolled over and touched me. I groaned in pleasure, swelling to insane levels. Jade's hand was firm and confident, and I didn't stand a chance. I had been far too worked up to begin with and her unexpected change took me by surprise.

"Jade, stop. I'm going to come if you keep that up."

She laughed. "That's kind of the point. You looked a little, well, uncomfortable."

My mate was trying to take care of my needs. It was crazy. We still barely knew each other, yet we were so in tune, so connected. That turned me on almost as much as what her hand was doing to me.

She leaned down and started kissing my chest, tasting and licking the various planes and textures. It was too much. I suddenly understood why she'd stopped me early to regroup. The sensations were overstimulating, and I released hard without warning, surprising us both.

As my body tightened and convulsed as I tried to gain control of myself, she sat up and smirked proudly at me.

"I'm not some two-pump chump. I swear I'm not," I insisted not absolutely certain that wouldn't be the case with her.

She giggled. "I tried to tell you the bond makes everything more."

"Point made. Jesus, I've never come that fast before. It's embarrassing."

She seemed proud of herself for being the cause of that.

"We're even now," she said.

She took the edge of the blanket and carefully cleaned me up. Her simple care was almost as much of a turn on as earlier. I wondered if it would always be like this for us, effortless. I'd seen others fight their bond. Or the bond caused them to act irrationally like the time Damon tried to attack some of us brothers. I didn't feel like that. I felt perfectly at peace and accepting of my bond with Jade.

"You know, the fastest way to stop the rumors would be to just tell people we're mated," I said.

"That will only encourage the rumors further and you know it," she insisted.

"Maybe, but they'd at least be different rumors and I wouldn't have to hear how much you hate me around every corner, or how you're plotting revenge to ruin the party this weekend."

"Oh, that's a real thing. I mean, payback's only fair, right?" she said with a straight face and I couldn't discern if she was being serious or joking. "I mean, did you or did you not get shit faced and crowd surf naked at my party?"

I sighed. "I did, but that was mostly your fault."

"How was any of that my fault?"

"You dropped a bomb on me and then disappeared. I tried to find you, but you were just gone. I'd just been hit with the mating call, realized my mate was my biggest enemy, and you just left. I was dealing with it the best way I could."

She laughed. "So little ole me is your biggest enemy now?"

"Definitely."

"Do you always kiss your enemies?"

I smirked. "My father told me to keep my enemies close." I reached down and pulled her tightly to my side as she rolled and rested on my chest. "Think this is close enough?"

She snorted. "I doubt that's what he had in mind."

Jade
Chapter 15

Brett and I had stayed up late again as we laid there talking. I got back to my dorm around five in the morning, long enough for a few hours of sleep before I needed to get up and start the day.

The majority of my classes were on Monday/Wednesday/Friday, so I'd be busy all afternoon. I felt almost giddy with happiness. For the girl who rarely smiled, that was a huge change. I couldn't keep the grin off my face every time I thought of Brett, which was like every second.

He was nothing like I'd imagined he'd be, and everything I needed. I'd never been this happy or content in life. I had never given much thought to my true mate. I'd never even really believed in the stories, chalking them up to little more than fairytales, but it was all real.

I walked through my day trying to hold my usual invisible persona, but it wasn't working. It was like the veil had been torn down and everyone was taking notice of me. It made me feel vulnerable and I didn't like it.

Maybe I was putting off mating pheromones or something because of Brett, because for the first time since I'd started at the ARC, guys were beginning to pay attention to me, and I didn't really understand why.

Personally, I loved my look despite what everyone, including my mother, thought of it. The piercings, the tattoos, they were all special to me. I dyed my hair because I loved the splash of color to my otherwise drab world.

The problem now was that my world didn't feel so drab and colorless. I dressed in the same clothes I always wore, but I felt different, more confident, more beautiful. I could only guess it showed through now. I wasn't used to the attention. Unlike some girls, I didn't really care for it either.

"Hey, it's Jade right?" a guy asked as I was standing in line to order pizza in the cafeteria. I almost always ate in the cafeteria simply because it was the best deal and my meal plan was already paid for.

"Yeah," I said, hoping my tone would tell him to back off without me having to actually say the words.

"I'm Darren, it's nice to finally meet you. I've been wanting to introduce myself for a while. I think it's really cool how you're standing up the fascists on Greek Row."

This time last week I would have probably squealed and kissed this guy. By all outward appearances he was exactly my type. He was good looking enough and wearing all black. His hair was even dyed black and he had heavy black eyeliner around his eyes and several visible piercings.

"That's not really what I'm about," I tried to explain to him though I didn't want to waste my time and energy trying too hard because while to the outside world we probably looked like a perfect couple, in my heart I was already claimed.

I knew the second Brett walked in. I could feel his presence as if he were standing next to me. I glanced across the room just as he entered. He was wearing khaki pants and a dark green polo. He looked nothing like me or this guy Darren. I guess opposites really could attract.

I spotted Kaitlyn with him and abruptly excused myself from a potentially awkward situation, telling Darren my friend had just arrived. I left before he could even think about inviting himself along.

Kaitlyn was with Brett and his friends, but I used her as an excuse anyway. I could feel the frustration coming off him in waves the closer I got. I was certain he'd seen me talking to Darren. It was nothing, but Brett was jealous, and I loved it. There was something seriously sexy about my perfect mate on the verge of losing it.

If anyone was watching it looked like I stepped up and cut Brett off as I spoke to Kaitlyn. In reality, I knew he needed reassurance that I was okay before he really did something stupid. He had mentioned something earlier about some of his friends losing it during their mating period. I suspected he was just as close.

I managed to brush up against him in the process of getting to Kaitlyn, and he relaxed almost instantly.

"Everything okay?" he asked in a low voice.

"Nothing I can't handle. He was praising me for taking down the fascist Greeks," I said as if I were telling Kaitlyn.

She laughed. "Seriously?"

"Seriously."

"What did you say to that?"

"That he was clueless and that wasn't what I was trying to do."

"You're not?" Jackson asked hopefully.

I turned to look at him. I knew who he was, but we had never really met before.

"I'm not trying to take down the Greek system. Maybe I considered it once, but that's not my purpose. I just want everyone here at the ARC to feel like they belong and are part of something. I get that you guys already have that with your brotherhood, but that's often at the expense of excluding the rest of us, and often through ridicule and embarrassment even." At least he had the good grace to look a little embarrassed by that. "I just want to see that change. I'm not trying to take away your family or your house. There's room for all of us here at the ARC if we can just learn to be respectful and accepting of each other."

Another guy spoke up. He had an Australian accent. "So you're a little socialist demanding equality for everyone? Because that's not how the real world works little girl."

Kaitlyn's eyes went wide, and I felt Brett on the edge of attack. To his credit he managed to keep his cool while the entire incident only caused minor attention.

"Stand down Lachlan," Brett said through gritted teeth with an edge to his voice I'd never heard before.

I instinctively took a step back towards him. His hand went to my hip as discreetly as possible to calm himself. While where we were standing shielded me from the rest of the cafeteria, Lachlan definitely noticed.

"What the hell is going on?" he asked.

Jackson looked to Brett for permission before he spoke. Out of the corner of my eye I saw him nod.

"Emergency meeting at the doghouse tonight. Spread the word. All brothers are required to attend. I don't give a shit if you have a class or not. Are we clear?" Jackson said.

Several of the guys nodded without another word.

"Lachlan," Jackson started.

"I'm cool," he said watching Brett and I carefully.

"Well this was fun. Come on Jade, let's go eat before these morons spoil our meal," Kaitlyn said.

As I turned to follow her, I got a good look at Brett. He still looked a little wild, but calmer than when he had first arrived.

"Are you okay?" I mouthed.

He smiled and gave me a nod of reassurance.

Before anyone really noticed the interaction, besides Lachlan and Jackson who were watching us both closely, I walked away.

Once at the table Kaitlyn sighed. "Not exactly how either of us wanted to introduce you to the boys. They'll come around."

I sighed. "Just a clear reminder of just how screwed up this all is," I muttered.

How could I go from feeling so great this morning to so bad and out of place now? I saw the look Lachlan had shared with Brett. He thought Brett had lost his mind supporting me, and he hadn't even really spoken up and said anything at all as he was just trying to control his own emotions.

It only took a few minutes of us being seated before Darren walked over asking to join us.

"Sorry, we really have some girl stuff to discuss that would only be awkward for you," Kaitlyn said sweetly.

"Oh, I have sisters. I don't mind," he said, setting his tray next to mine and lowering himself into the booth beside me.

"Seriously?" I asked. "We aren't trying to hurt your feelings, we just really would like some privacy to talk."

Another guy walked over and took the seat next to Kaitlyn. He looked stoned. "Dudes." He gave us all a head nod and sat down.

"Slash, this is Jade, Jade, Slash," Darren said.

Kaitlyn was trying not to laugh at their audacity.

"We saw how those fascists were trying to gang up on you. You're safe with us, Jade," Darren assured me.

I heard a growl and looked up, surprised to find Lachlan standing at our table. "The ladies said they wanted to be left alone. I suggest you get your heads out of your asses and abide by that request."

I could feel Brett's anger rising and had expected to find him there, not Lachlan. I looked over at the table I knew they always sat at. Jackson and another guy I hadn't met yet each had an arm around him physically restraining him in his seat.

Darren and Slash stood up to Lachlan.

"We aren't the ones the ladies need protection from you asshole. So walk away before this gets ugly."

Lachlan looked back towards his brothers seeing the effort it was taking to restrain Brett, and I realized that not even fully knowing the situation, this guy would do anything for my mate.

"Come on Kaitlyn. I'm not feeling very hungry right now. Let's just leave," I suggested.

"Fine," she said as we both scooted until the intruders finally moved. Lachlan stayed in a stare down with them until we were safely out of the way.

I went to the trash to throw away my tray.

"Screw that," Kaitlyn said, handing me a to go container. I smiled gratefully at her and quickly filled it. She grabbed us two plastic forks and napkins, and we left with our food.

When we got outside, she handed me her box and pulled out her phone to type a message.

"Come on," she said, leading me into the woods.

We didn't walk as far as the place Brett and I usually met, but there was a nice pretty clearing beside the lake much lower down. It was a popular picnic area during the weekends and warm weather.

Today was dreary and overcast. It looked like it could start storming at any second, so the area was deserted. I picked the table closest to the water and sat down, opening the lid and finally enjoying my food.

I only got two bites in before I felt a familiar tingling sensation that caused goosebumps to break out all over. Brett,

Jackson, Lachlan, and two others I didn't know soon entered the clearing.

Brett didn't hesitate to join me at the table. He set his stuff down and his hand immediately started rubbing my back.

"Are you okay?" I finally asked, assuming by his actions that it was safe to talk openly.

He leaned over and took a deep breathe, then kissed my forehead. "I am now."

"Bloody hell. When did this happen?" Lachlan asked as he sat next to Kaitlyn.

The other three guys pulled another table closer to ours and sat down too.

"The bonfire," Kaitlyn said. "Why do you think he got so wasted? I mean seriously, when was the last time you saw Brett drink himself senseless?"

Lachlan considered that for a moment. "Never."

"Freshman year," Jackson and one of the other guys said in unison.

"It only happened once, and Brett swore he'd never lose control like that again," Jackson added. "Of course, we all know who you are, but I'm not sure we've actually met," he said to me.

"You're Jackson, right?" I asked.

He grinned. "Yeah. It's nice to finally meet you, Jade. This is Neal and Chad."

Neal was the other guy that had answered with Jackson. I was certain I'd never seen him around before.

"Chad? You're Ember's mate?" I asked.

He perked up and smiled. "Yeah. Do you know Ember?"

"We had a girls' day at Karis's yesterday," Kaitlyn told him.

"She did mention something like that, but didn't tell me she'd met Jade," he said.

"I think she was a little salty that you hadn't told her," Kaitlyn said with a shrug.

"Wait, you guys knew?" Lachlan questioned.

"Knew what?" Neal asked.

"That Brett and Jade were mated," Lachlan informed him.

Neal looked at us both in surprise. "You are?"

Everyone burst out laughing. It was definitely the stress reliever we all needed. I could feel a lot of the tension lift, and Brett finally relaxed.

"Remember what I said last night?" he whispered to me.

I laughed. "Not feeling so confident about not losing it now?"

"Something like that."

"I'm sorry about that. I swear, I don't even know who those guys were."

"Really? They looked like friends of yours," Neal said. The guys all stared at him. "What? I'm just saying that they looked like the kinds of people Jade would attract or be friends with is all."

Brett growled at him, but Neal just dismissed it. I got the feeling he was a bit of an airhead.

"Jade doesn't have friends. She just has me," Kaitlyn said sweetly. I noticed she used that tone around these guys a lot. I still didn't really know what her deal was with the doghouse.

"So, are you two like official then?" Lachlan asked.

"Define official," I inquired.

Brett grinned. "She's going to be an awesome lawyer someday."

"I guess I mean like are you two really mates? Like true mates? Is it public knowledge? Are we the last to know?" Lachlan asked. He seemed upset at that thought.

"Yes, Jade is my one true mate," Brett said. There was something so profound in him openly saying it to his brothers. "No, we have not gone public yet."

"Why not?" Neal asked. Yup, he was completely oblivious.

"Because of all the rumors and shit flying around, but that is likely a huge mistake, dude. I mean with the party this weekend and everything," Jackson said.

"Hate to say it, but Jackson's right. There are going to be a lot of unmated males there, Brett. You barely held it together today when that guy started flirting with her. You're going to do something stupid, so just come clean so everyone knows to be aware of it," Chad added.

He looked to me for the right answer.

I shrugged. "I don't know. Maybe they're right," I said.

"Really? You were so adamant that we keep everything quiet," he reminded me.

"That's because no one will believe it," Neal said. "Everyone will talk shit and come to the conclusion that all this drama was a ploy to further boost Greek Row's control, and Jade was in on it the entire time. Her credibility will be shot," Neal said. Maybe not quite the idiot I suspected.

"That's not going to happen," Kaitlyn said, dismissing him entirely.

"Is that what you're afraid of?" Brett asked me.

I shrugged again. "That thought may have crossed my mind."

"What? That's crazy Neal talk, Jade. Don't listen to it. I'll run cleanup on this. It'll be fine. Go public already," Kaitlyn insisted.

Lachlan shook his head. "You two look as different as night and day. It's crazy, and yet, I can see it. Let me guess, Jade, you're some form of cat-shifter, right?"

Brett snorted. "I was convinced of that at first too."

"What? Why?" I asked.

"Because you're complete opposites. It has to be cats and dogs. It's just too priceless," Lachlan added.

I shook my head. "I'm not a damn cat."

"Fine," Lachlan pouted. "What are you then?"

"She's a coyote, dude. We're actually a lot more alike than even we suspected," Brett said.

He had finished his meal while we talked. Putting down his fork, he reached for my hand under the table and linked our fingers together. I felt stupid over how happy that simple gesture made me.

Brett

Chapter 16

I was glad she didn't pull away or try to deny our bond when I took her hand. I was still worried she would. Everything was happening so fast, and yet it felt like we'd known each other forever.

I was grateful to Jackson for stepping in and defusing a potentially bad situation. True, there were some coyote hotheads, but I had never been one of them. I was calm and diplomatic. Sure, I'd kill to protect my boys and my family, and that most definitely included Jade now. But I didn't just fly off the handle over nothing. So what if some guy talked to my girl?

The real problem was that that guy looked the part next to her so much more than I ever could. I didn't want to change to fit into Jade's life, and I would never dream of asking her to change for me. I liked her just the way she was. There wasn't a single hair on her head that I would change, unless she wanted to turn those purple or red or something, and I would be fine with that too.

I couldn't be the goth in black or the emo wearing his emotions on his sleeve walking around looking depressed all the time. Those guys weren't me and never would be.

Jade must have sensed my anxiety building up again as she gave my hand a squeeze and leaned closer to me. Her brief touches in the lunchroom had saved me from making a colossal ass of myself. I didn't want to be that guy either.

It was far more important than any of that, though. I was Jade's true mate, and none of those other guys could ever compare to that. I realized I not only wanted to claim her publicly, but in every other way possible too.

After lunch I asked Jade if I could walk her to her class. She hesitantly said yes. I knew it was a big step for us. I hadn't even told all my brothers about us yet, though that would be rectified later tonight.

We said goodbye to my friends and strolled through the woods. No one cared or noticed us as we walked across campus until we hit the quad. We weren't holding hands or doing anything to draw attention, but just like over the weekend, the second someone took notice and got excited all cell phones were pointed at the two of us.

Some guy recording everything started asking questions and shoving his phone in Jade's face. Clearly he was an overenthusiastic communications major with a confidence that would ensure he would be sporting a permanent black eye.

"Jade, is it true that Brett threatened you in the cafeteria today and that's why you left in tears?" he asked.

"I didn't leave in tears," she insisted.

"An eyewitness named Slash said the doghouse surrounded you and became defensive and forced you to leave."

"I'm pretty sure Slash was so high he probably saw a purple elephant serving salad too," she chided.

"What about the death threats you've been receiving Brett?" the guy persisted.

"What the hell are you talking about?" I demanded. "Is that some kind of threat from you?"

"No, no man, I'm just here to report the news," he insisted.

"You don't want news, or at least not the truth," Jade said. "You're gossip news and nothing more. The truth doesn't matter to you at all."

"Jade, I'm on your side here. I'm trying to help," he said.

"How exactly?" she asked.

Someone else responded. "He's on a mission to make the Greeks look bad. He thinks that's what you want, Jade."

"That is not what I want, so stop it," she scolded.

A text went off on my phone. I glanced down at it. It was from Dean Shannahan. A meeting with the administration had been called and I was required to attend. It was scheduled for Thursday evening. I responded that I'd be there and turned back to the chaos unfolding before me.

I had to get Jade out of here.

I grabbed her by the arm to lead her away. "Excuse us, no time for questions. Jade is late to class."

I didn't stop as I plowed through the group and growled at the few that tried to follow. They backed off when they realized I wasn't messing around.

I did not like the feeling of being trapped, but I especially didn't like Jade being trapped by those morons. We didn't give them a story, and no one seemed to question why I was walking her to class.

I took a deep breath and let her scent soothe me.

"It'll all die down soon," I assured her.

She nodded. "Did you get a text about the administration meeting tomorrow night?"

"Yeah, you too?"

"I did. I saw you look at your phone the same time mine went off. It's weird that after everything they finally decide to call us in together."

I shrugged. "About time if you ask me. Do you want to have dinner tonight?"

"I thought you called a meeting at the doghouse."

"I did, but that's not until seven. You're welcome to come for it if you'd like."

I was disappointed when she shook her head.

"Baby steps, Brett. I think you should be the one to fill them in. I don't even know them. It would just be awkward. I'm sure they'll have plenty to say about it," she said.

"That's why it would be nice to have you there. They'd likely be nicer about it, and I wouldn't have to hurt anyone tonight," I told her honestly. I knew all the shit I'd said about Jade before I knew who she was to me, and I knew that my brothers did, too. They were not going to let me live that down.

"Sorry, you're on your own," she said. "I have to run, and I'll be in class until six. It often runs late, so I probably shouldn't try to squeeze in dinner before your meeting. I'll talk to you later."

She was off and running before I could get another word in.

I had two afternoon classes that I couldn't begin to recall a single word mentioned in. Then I met Jackson for dinner.

"We haven't named pledges for this year yet," he reminded me. "Those same five guys that have been hanging around all semester were at the house when I announced the mandatory meeting. They asked if they could come. I told them it was brothers only, but I won't be surprised if they show up. I think they believe if they keep showing up and hanging out that we'll forget they aren't already brothers and admit them."

I shrugged. "They seem cool enough. We still need to take a vote, but I think we're probably all in agreement that we'd pick them anyway."

"Yeah, as much as I don't want to admit it, you're right about that."

"We can add that to the agenda tonight too, take some of the heat off me," I said.

"Fat chance of that," Jackson laughed.

After we finished eating, we walked home to wait for everyone to arrive.

I guess I shouldn't have been surprised, but the first five to arrive were Asher, Dylan, Finn, and the twins, Holden and Hudson, our five most aggressive rushers ever.

"Guys, it's a fraternity meeting. You're not supposed to be here," I explained as their faces fell with disappointment. "Look, what the hell. You can hang out in Chad's room with the dampener on while I start the meeting and I'll come and get you if it's okay for you to be there. Deal?"

They all happily agreed and rushed Chad's room ahead of the brothers' arrival. The problem was, Ember was in there studying and they nearly scared the daylight out of her.

"Brett!" Ember yelled.

I sighed and peeked my head in. "Please Ember, just for a few minutes. I don't know what else to do with them."

"They aren't brothers. They aren't even pledges," she pointed out. "Send them home."

"But we really want to be," Asher said hopefully. The others all nodded.

She relented and let them stay. I was relieved that by the time I got back to the common room everyone was there. Word had already spread through the house, but they all wanted to hear it directly from me.

"Hey guys. I'm glad you're all here on time for once. We have a couple pieces of business to address and then I want to talk to you guys about what's been going on with me."

They all respectfully kept their questions to themselves as I called the group to order, quickly went through the standard D.O.G. meeting requirements, and got down to business.

"First, we haven't chosen pledges for this year yet. I have to tell you, in Chad's room right now are the five most aggressive rushers I've ever seen, waiting to join this group, like right now, tonight."

The guys laughed because they all knew exactly who I was talking about.

"What the hell?" Chad chimed in.

"Just let them in," Neal said.

"Let them pledge," someone else corrected.

"Everyone's here let's just vote on it," another recommended.

"Okay, we need to do this the right way, so I'll call their names one by one and you can vote aloud. Deal?" I asked.

"Yeah, second," Jackson said. It had been his idea anyway.

"Finn, yay or nay?" I asked.

"Yay," they unanimously said.

"Asher?"

"Yay."

"Dylan?"

"Yay."

"Hudson?"

"Yay."

"Holden?"

"Nay," they all said.

I stopped and stared at them. "You're turning down one twin and not the other? They're brothers."

Jackson laughed. "He's also the sneaky little bastard listening in from the kitchen."

Holden peeked his head out apologetically. "Hey guys, what's going on?"

"Would you please get your ass back in the room?" I begged. "I said I needed a few minutes. I'm trying man."

Once I was certain he was in the room I asked again.

"Last time. Holden?"

"Yay," they all said.

"Anyone have any problems with them just joining us tonight?"

"Your show, boss," Jackson said. The others all nodded.

I excused myself and walked over to Chad's room. "Finn, Asher, Hudson, and Dylan. You guys are all in, come on out and join us. You'll be getting official pledge offers soon."

Hudson held back and stared at his brother. "What about Holden?"

I shook my head. "Sorry man, Holden's. . ."

"If Holden's not in, neither am I," Hudson said firmly. "I could never do that to my brother."

The other three all sighed and went to stand beside him.

"We stand with Holden too. All or nothing. That's what brothers do," Dylan said.

I shook my head. They were serious and definitely were going to be a pain in my ass all year long, but that solid brotherhood was what the doghouse was all about.

"Well, good thing we voted Holden in too. Now all five of you get your asses out there."

They took a moment to turn to each other and celebrate before excitedly joining the brothers in the common room.

Ember laughed at me as I shook my head and said a quick prayer for sanity before following behind them.

Everyone quieted the second I walked back into the room. I was certainly used to having all eyes on me at these sorts of meetings, but tonight was different because I knew they were waiting for me to tell them about Jade. It was personal, and that brought a vulnerability I wasn't used to.

"Okay, well, you guys be sure to welcome our first batch of pledges for the new freshman class. We won't be holding an official ceremony tonight, but they are unofficially in. I'm not sure the history of the doghouse has ever seen a more dedicated pledge class."

Everyone laughed knowing those five had immersed themselves into our lives one hundred percent since the second they stepped foot on the ARC. I think a few of the guys weren't sure if they were rushing or transferring brothers, they had been that involved.

"Well, if no one has anything else for tonight, I think we can officially adjourn this meeting," I said.

"Hold up, you're not getting off that easy. I believe you have an announcement to make about a certain sometimes blue-haired gal with big green eyes who always dresses in black," Connor pointed out.

"If it's alright with you guys, I'd like to have that talk not on our official transcript meeting."

"I'll second adjourning," Jackson said. I nodded a thanks his way. I could always count on Jackson to have my back.

"Third," Chad said. "All those who agree say yay."

"Yay."

"Close enough, official meeting over," Chad told them and put away the notes he had been taking.

"So, Jade?" Connor pressed.

I smiled just at the mention of her name. "Some of you are already aware of this, and this may come as a shock to others, but Jade Michaels is my one true mate."

"Seriously?" Tyler asked.

"Holy shit, I did not see that coming," Pete said.

"You and Jade? Really? I don't see it," Brian added.

I gave them a few minutes to absorb what I said.

"But she hates us. She's doing everything in her power to take down Greek Row," Reid said loud enough to silence the room.

"She's not," I said confidently.

"But she is," he insisted. "Remember, in case Kaitlyn couldn't get close to her, which we all know backfired on us miserably seeing as she's Jade's new BFF, I also attended the little rally she threw." He pulled a folded-up piece of paper from his pocket. "Here I even wrote it down. This is a direct quote from her during the rally. "Since the beginning of Archibald Reynolds the elitist pricks segregate themselves from the rest of us as they sit up in their fancy houses and throw elaborate, invite-only parties. This is the twenty-first century. We are striving for an inclusive society which goes against everything the Greeks stand for." Now does that sound like someone that is on our side?"

Murmurs started throughout the room as people lowered their voices to talk to the guy next to them.

"Settle down," I said as they slowly tuned back to me. "Look, maybe that was her goal, but I just told you, she's my mate. She can't hurt me, and to take down Greek Row, to destroy this, would hurt me. Plus, you guys know, mate or not, I'm never letting that happen. You guys are my family." They started whooping and cheering.

"Dude, she's your mate, that's easier said than done," Chad said.

I nodded. "I know that, Chad. Trust me, I know." Everyone quieted again to hear what I was going to say. "And I know I said a lot of shit about Jade, but that was before I knew her. Before I knew who she was to me. I'm just asking each of you to forget about all that and give her a chance. Do it for me. This is going to work out, I promise you guys that. No one is taking our home or breaking up our brotherhood."

Jade

Chapter 17

It was raining, but I didn't want to miss Brett, so I grabbed my rain jacket and headed for our spot a little before midnight. No one was out around campus and the air was crisp as the rain bit into me, stinging my face.

When I arrived at the clearing, I knew instantly he wasn't there yet, so I waited, standing there looking out into the dark as the rain continued to pour down. I considered shifting into my coyote form knowing it would be warmer, but it was too cold to strip, and I didn't want to ruin my clothes.

I had never felt so alone out there in the dark. A sort of sad emptiness set in as midnight came and went and I realized Brett wasn't coming. Still I waited on, just in case. I gave it until one in the morning before slowly making my way back home.

I felt like a complete fool. It was raining and we hadn't even officially made plans to meet up. I knew he had that meeting with his brothers. He'd asked if I wanted to go with him and I'd been the one to say no.

The desperation I felt needing to see him scared the shit out of me. I missed him. I tried to tell myself that I barely knew him so that wasn't even possible, but I was just lying to myself. I may not have known him all that long, but he'd just swooped into my life. I was so overcome by the emotions the bond had stirred in me, that I hadn't truly stopped to acknowledge the impact rationally. I'd just blindly accepted it as fact. Brett and I were meant to be together, despite the glaringly obvious signs that screamed we shouldn't be.

I never took anything for blind faith, so this realization was freaking me out. I checked my cell phone a hundred times on the walk back, but there was nothing. I knew I had never given him my number. Why hadn't I? Why hadn't he given me his?

I had asked him not to make a public scene about us. I didn't want people to know. But he was with his brothers telling them all anyway. What did that really say about the chances of a relationship with him?

By the time I'd made it back to my dorm, I'd already convinced myself that it would be in my best interest to forget Brett Evans even existed. We hadn't known each other for even a week and while the two nights we'd spent up late talking and fooling around had been amazing, there were more important things in my future than a boy, even a mate.

Mine, a voice growled in my head.

No, he wasn't mine. My coyote would grow to understand that in time. Besides, we'd be too busy preparing for graduation and then on to law school to even have time for Brett.

With that thought in mind, I made a rash decision. I pulled out my laptop and I logged on. I already had a link saved to three of the best law schools in the nation. I had only actually applied to the ARC. I knew Brett was also planning to stay on for higher education, so I bit the bullet and I pulled up the application for Harvard, and then on to the next, and the next. This gave me options and made me feel better about myself as I finished up just before the sun was rising. The tears came out of nowhere as I started to cry. For what? I wasn't certain, but I didn't try to stop it and soon drifted off to sleep.

It was late afternoon before I awoke again. I'd slept through my alarm and missed all of my classes for the day as the last one was just beginning and there was no way I could get ready and make it across campus for even an acceptable late arrival.

With a groan of frustration, I rolled over onto my back and stared at the ceiling. It was quiet. No one would come looking for me or even think to check on me. I was no one.

Feeling broken and incomplete with my life, I dragged myself out of bed. I desperately needed to do laundry, and my closet was down to the bare minimum, or basically the clothes my mother bought every time she visited and insisted I needed a little color in my life.

With a sigh, I pulled out a pair of dark denim skinny jeans and a tie-dye T-shirt. It looked like something I might wear to garden with Mom at home. She was a free spirit and loved colors. The brighter the better. I smiled just a little thinking of her.

Knowing my usual combat boots wouldn't cut it with this outfit, I dusted off a pair of navy vans hidden in the back of my closet.

I went to the bathroom and scrubbed off the mess on my face from where I had cried myself to sleep. I looked at the pile of makeup on the sink and just frowned at myself in the mirror. I grabbed a hair tie and threw my shoulder length hair into a short ponytail, grabbed my keys and cell phone, and left before I could talk myself out of it.

I never left the house without my full armor solidified in my appearance. Dressing like a normal, average college student left me feeling even more vulnerable and out of place. It didn't matter. I walked quickly to the parking lot and doubted anyone bothered to notice me.

Once I passed through the gates to Archibald Reynold's, I let myself relax a little. I drove for a couple of hours, finally settling on a park about forty-five minutes away. It was thick and lush with trails amongst the giant trees.

I parked the car and got out. I walked the trails just thinking about everything that was happening and trying to get my priorities straight. I decided that the inclusion project would just have to be someone else's legacy. I needed some space and time alone. Everything happening was just too much and too out of character for me.

By the time I got back to the car my stomach was growling. I hadn't eaten all day. I also didn't have enough money to stop along the way, so I drove straight back to the ARC with new perspectives in check.

A little less than half an hour out, my phone beeped. I took a second and glanced down at the screen, even knowing I shouldn't while behind the wheel. It was the reminder for my meeting with the administration. I got a sick feeling in my stomach.

A text chimed and I pulled over to check it. It was from Dean Shannahan, personally verifying that I would be there. I couldn't tell him no, so I responded with a yes and got back on the road. I drove faster than I should as I was in a time crunch now. I wasn't looking forward to telling them about my decision, but it had to be done.

I was going to be late, so I parked the car as close as possible and sprinted towards the building they were expecting me in. Before I even reached the door, I smelled him. Brett. I had completely forgotten he would be there too. I wasn't prepared for this.

Taking a deep breath and finding my resolve, I turned the doorknob and walked purposefully into the room. I knew he was watching me, but I didn't even allow myself to make eye contact with him. Instead I marched over to the furthest seat from him and sat between two of my professors, crossing my arms over my chest.

Dean Shannahan stared at me in surprise. "Jade?"

"Yes?" I asked glancing down at my watch. "I'm sorry I'm a few minutes late."

"No, it's fine, it's just, well, never mind," he said.

"Just what?" I asked.

He shuffled awkwardly from one foot to the other. "You just look so different today. Must be the hair."

I looked down at my jeans and T-shirt and blushed furiously. I had forgotten I was wearing normal clothes for once. Of course that would look out of character for me.

I sighed. "I forgot we were having this meeting today. You caught me off-campus, hiking."

He nodded and smiled as if that explained everything and continued. "Well, as you know, we have quite the rivalry going on between Ms. Michaels and Mr. Evans."

"There is no rivalry," I blurted out. "The Greek houses are opening up to host an inclusive party this weekend and I have faith they'll continue to be more welcoming in the future, sir. I will not be pursuing anything further."

I got up to excuse myself. I already felt my resolve weakening and I hadn't even looked in Brett's direction, though I could feel his presence and it was hard to ignore.

"Just a minute, Jade," Professor Rodgers said. I'd had him for accounting and pre-law. He was nice enough, but when he grabbed my arm to stop me from leaving, I had to hold back a growl and force restraint on my coyote to keep from lashing out at him. "This doesn't sound like you at all. Did someone get to you? Are you being threatened?" he asked.

I stared at him, truly looking at him for the first time and I sniffed the air around us. There was an odd scent coming off of him, but somehow, I knew he wasn't a shifter. He was a human. All faculty and staff at the ARC were supposed to be shifters. This realization hit me hard and I didn't know how to process it, but I had to get out of there and quick.

"No one is threatening me," I said. "I just think the bonfire did its job, and the message has been heard. I see the changes already occurring and so my job is done."

Professor Jordan was on my other side. She had returned this semester after an extended maternity leave. "Jade, there's still so much more to be done."

"Why are you guys pressuring her on this?" Brett asked.

I saw an evil smirk cross Jordan's face as she smiled sweetly in his direction.

"No pressure, Mr. Evans. We just happen to agree with the stance Jade took on inclusion and want to encourage her to strive towards that vision."

I leaned over and sniffed. It was the same chemically scent wafting off Rodgers. Human? If I didn't know any better, I'd swear I was high and assessing the situation wrong. But since I wasn't, the hair on my arms stood up.

The comments that ensued seemed to pit Brett and I against each other. They didn't know we were true mates and that it wasn't going to work. After a few minutes of arguments throughout the room. I caved, just to see their reactions.

"You're right, Professor," I told Rodgers. "Inclusion is important but arguing about it is only causing further divisions here. I'm sure you can see that." He eyed me suspiciously, but I ignored it and continued. "I forget, what kind of shifter are you?"

He smiled. "Coyote."

"Really?" I asked. I knew for certain he was lying now, even as he nodded.

"Great, so am I," I said, and he blanched as his eyes darted around the room. "Perhaps we should end this argument the coyote way then?"

"Splendid idea," he said.

I dared a quick look at Brett who was quite confused.

"Very well, Sunday then on the quad," I said. "As the eldest coyote, you'll represent on the side of inclusion." I smiled happily at him then turned to Brett as I rose and headed for the door. "Mr. Evans, pick your champion. I have no doubt that Professor Rodger's coyote can take down any opponent you chose." I dared a quick wink at him and left the room.

Within seconds Brett was running out of the room to catch up with me.

"What the hell was that all about?" he asked. "What's this coyote way? You can't possibly mean a battle to the death to settle this."

I laughed, the light hysterical kind. In truth I was terrified. Why were there humans in positions of authority at the ARC? This place was supposed to be a safe haven for shifters.

"Not here," I said.

"Tonight?" he asked.

I snorted. "Seriously? After you didn't even bother to show last night?"

"What? I had a meeting with the brothers last night. You knew that."

"At what? Seven?" I said.

Brett grabbed my arm and spun me around. My coyote responded just as strongly as she did when Rodgers had grabbed my arm in the room, but this time it wasn't a cold, uncomfortable feeling, but the exact opposite. My entire body warmed to his touch and I cursed my body's reaction to him.

"Were you waiting at our spot last night, Jade? In the rain?" I didn't answer so he kept talking. "Jesus. It was pouring out there. I almost went for a run just to feel a little closer to you. Jackson stopped me because the weather was so bad." He growled trying to get himself together.

"It doesn't matter," I told him. I wanted to turn and leave, afraid I might even cry. I had spent all day getting a grip on my emotions and he broke down that barrier in a matter of minutes.

Instead of leaving, I found myself reaching out and placing my hands on his chest. His body instantly relaxed and he regained control of himself. It was a heady feeling knowing I had that much power over him.

"What's with this look today?" he asked, crinkling up his nose as if he didn't like it.

I looked down at myself. "What? You have something against normal clothes?"

He frowned. "It's not you."

"I would think that would be a positive thing for you," I murmured looking over the squeaky-clean cut image he projected with his khakis and polo, neatly tucked in with belt and everything.

"Why would you think that? I like how you look. You don't have to change a thing for me."

Dammit. Why was he saying all the right things? I cleared my throat nervously and shrugged. "I need to do laundry," I confessed.

"And this?" he asked, tugging on my ponytail.

I sighed. "I really was off campus hiking today."

"By yourself?" he asked. I could feel his Alpha nature surge, as if I needed protection.

I snorted. "Yeah."

His jaw locked tightly as he looked around. He nodded towards Greek Row for me to follow him. I looked around noting there were quite a few people nearby, but no one was paying attention to us. They'd have to do a double take to even notice it was me.

I shook my head, but he growled low in warning for me to follow and kept walking.

I threw my arms up in exasperation and went against my better judgement.

We didn't talk at all on the way to the doghouse. I hadn't been there since my freshman year and the fiasco that had ensued there.

As we got to the front porch, the door opened, and Damon stood there. It was like déjà vu and I freaked, ready to run.

"Please, don't," Damon said. "I'll leave. I know how important it is for Brett to bring you here, Jade. Stay."

I looked up at Damon and saw the truth of his words in his eyes. Then I turned to Brett and he looked so hopeful. My heart lurched in my chest.

"You don't have to go," I told Damon. "It's fine."

He gave me that signature bad boy smirk of his and stepped aside for us to pass.

Brett nodded to a few guys lounging on couches in the living room. I recognized several of them, but only gave a weak smile at those that nodded or waved my way. Brett didn't stop as he headed down a hallway to the door at the end and opened it, holding it for me to pass through first.

I knew from the smell it was his room. "No roommate?" I asked.

He smirked. "There's got to be some perks to being president, doesn't there?"

I shrugged. "I guess," I said as I looked around trying to take it all in.

I stopped at a stack of CD's he had next to a stereo. It felt very old school. Most people would just have a playlist on their phone. I picked up a few and looked them over. He had a pretty wide selection, but the ones out were all hardcore. He had all my favorite bands represented.

"You actually listen to this stuff?" I asked not even bothering to hide my surprise.

"Don't judge before listening to it. It has some sick rhythms and the complexity of the music is astounding. I love it. Make fun all you want," he said a little defensively.

I laughed. "You? Really?"

I started laughing even harder at the thought of Brett at a concert for any of these bands. Where I may look like the one out of place around campus, he for sure would be the one to stand out there.

I sifted through and found one for Our Last Night. "No way! This is their new one. It hasn't even released yet. How did you get it?"

"You've heard of them?"

"Duh, they're one of my favorite bands!"

He smirked. "I'm friends with the drummer. He got me an early copy to check out."

"You do not know the drummer," I insisted.

"Seriously?" He sighed and pulled out his phone. Next thing I know the drummer from Our Last Night was talking to me on the screen. I'd seen him in concert a dozen times but had never been able to get close enough to even say hi. Now here he was. "Hi," I squeaked, and Brett laughed.

"Thanks man. Just proving my point," Brett said.

"That your girl?" he asked.

"Sure is."

"We'll be in town next month. Bring her on out," he said.

"I think I will. Send me some tickets. See you soon. Thanks." He hung up and gave me a smug grin. I was still in shock.

"Did you really just tell him to give you free tickets?"

Brett nodded. "Yeah, that okay with you?"

"What? Uh. . .I don't know!" I said. Just that morning I had been completely resolved to break things off with him. Now he was planning to take me to a concert in a month to see my favorite band. My brain couldn't reconcile this turn of events with my heart.

"Jade, sit," Brett commanded. "You look like you're going to hyperventilate."

"I might," I confessed.

Brett

Chapter 18

Not everyone understood my love of screamo but Jade clearly did. Her reaction to me calling Timothy was priceless. I'd have to remember to thank him. I think he scored me major points with my mate.

"You're getting me sidetracked. When you calm down, I need to know what the hell was going on in that meeting today. And did you know Rodgers is a coyote?"

Jade sobered back up quickly and shook her head. "A poor mistake on his part," she said sourly.

"How come? And what was all that bullshit you were spouting about challenges the coyote way? We don't do that shit, Jade. You know that."

"Yeah, and he should have too, Brett. He's not a coyote. He lied. Rodgers is human, I'm certain of it. That was just a test to confirm my suspicions."

"That's crazy, Jade. There aren't any humans at the ARC. This is a safe zone for us."

There was a light knock on the door just before it opened, and Chad peaked his head in. He put his finger to his mouth and signaled for us to follow him.

Jade and I looked at each other and she shrugged, then turned to follow Chad, curious as to what this was all about, I followed too.

He took us into his room and shut the door. Ember squealed and jumped up to hug Jade.

"Hey Ember," she said awkwardly patting her on the back. I could feel her discomfort.

"I'm so excited you decided to come here," Ember gushed.

Jade rolled her eyes towards me. "He growled at me and didn't exactly give me a choice."

I was trying not to grin and shot her an irritated look instead, then let my frustrations out on Chad instead. "Dude, we're busy, what the hell is this all about?"

"There's a dampener in here. There's not in your room. You can't just blurt out something like that for everyone else to hear. You'll start a freaking riot and you know it."

"You heard us talking about my suspicions about Rodgers?" Jade asked.

"Yeah and that's not something I can afford to have spreading around campus," he surprised me by saying. Chad's eyes darted around the room everywhere but in my direction. He was hiding something. I was certain of it.

"What do you know?" I demanded.

"What's going on?" Ember asked, her excitement over seeing Jade dimming quickly.

"They know about Rodgers," Chad told her.

"Shit! Who else knows?" Ember asked.

"You mean Jade's suspicions are true?" I asked them both.

Ember turned and looked at Chad, then punched him in the arm. "Suspicions? Chad, they don't know anything."

"Sorry, I panicked. We can't afford for any suspicions to hang out there. And they were talking about him for just anyone walking by to hear."

"What do you know, Chad?" I asked again, a little firmer this time.

Ember sighed and shared a look with her mate. "You're going to have to tell them."

"I know I can trust him," Chad said. The way he said it insinuated that he couldn't trust Jade. That instantly pissed me off.

"She's my mate, Chad. I have no secrets from Jade. If you can trust me, then you trust her too. Now what the hell is going on?"

"Rodgers is a human. He's using some sort of chemical scent to try and cover that fact," Jade said.

"I'm really impressed you even caught on to that," Ember said with admiration evident in her voice.

"Professor Jordan and Dean Shannahan carry the same scent," she said.

Chad nodded. "Yeah, they take daily scent injections to try to mask themselves as one of us."

Ember was sitting at one of the two desks, and the rest of us were standing. I felt a little lightheaded trying to absorb the news, and then sat down hard onto their bed. I reached for Jade's hand and she slowly sat beside me. I felt like I was in shock with the news, but she was buzzing with energy and questions.

"They're part of some secret human faction, aren't they?" Jade asked, and I immediately thought she'd been watching too many movies. This was insane.

"Promise me nothing we say leaves this room and you will keep your mouth shut about any and all suspicions," Chad said directly to Jade.

She nodded seriously. "I promise." She elbowed me in the ribs.

"Yeah, yeah, I promise too," I said, still reeling in shock.

Chad got a strange look on his face and then his nose scrunched up. I'd seen it enough times to know he and Ember were doing their telepathy thing. For coyotes, like most canines, telepathy was one of the last stages of fully bonded mates, but each species was different, and squirrels were more vocal, so telepathy was their first stage in mating.

Ember didn't know that when it happened to them, and I'd had a front row seat when she had freaked out over it. Truth be told, I would have too, though there were moments when I'd give anything to know what was going through Jade's head.

A feeling of guilt hit me in the gut. She'd been out there all night, in the pouring rain, probably freezing just waiting on me. I didn't show. I'd let my mate down and hadn't even known it. I would do just about anything to make it up to her now.

Feeling frustrated with myself, I took it out on Chad and Ember. "Enough already, just tell us what's going on."

They both stopped and stared at me.

Jade looked back and forth between them. "What just happened?"

Chad and Ember didn't say a word.

"They were conferring with each other, either arguing about what to tell us or trying to get their story straight on how much to tell us. Just spill it already," I said to Chad.

"Wait, how long have you two been mated?" Jade asked.

"Almost a year," Chad admitted.

"But that's not possible. You have telepathy already?" she asked.

Ember shrugged. "Apparently that's normal for squirrel shifters."

"You're squirrels?" Jade asked sounding confused. "Both of you?" She looked at Chad. "But you live in the doghouse."

Chad laughed. "Yeah, I transferred here. Since I had already pledged Delta Omega Gamma back in the very human first college I attended, they automatically placed me here as a brother. Much to my surprise, they take the initials D.O.G. very serious here."

I laughed alongside Chad, remembering his first few days here as that reality had sunk in for us all. It was cool though. He was as much a D.O.G. as any of us.

"You must get a telepathic connection much sooner in the mating bond than we do. It's like the last stage for us, but you haven't been together long enough for a full bond," Jade observed.

"That would be correct," Chad confirmed.

"Wow. I guess I'd never really thought about it before and just assumed all bonds occurred the same way."

"I think we all assumed that before Chase and Jenna mated," I said.

"The wolf and the panther?" she asked.

"Yeah, that's right."

"I heard about them. I mean who didn't, right? It was a huge controversary all over campus."

I frowned. I hated knowing everyone was gossiping about my friends. Chase and Jenna had been through enough within their own families without having to face the prejudices around campus too.

She must have felt my discomfort because she reached out and touched my arm. It wasn't the first time she'd reacted that way. Earlier I had been certain she was pulling away from me. I don't know how I knew it, but I could sense it clearly. My coyote became agitated, and she had stepped up and placed her hands on my chest, instantly calming the beast within and settling my own nerves too. It sort of terrified me. We weren't bonded yet, and while in my heart Jade was already mine, there were moments where I felt a distance between us.

I suddenly realized how far off course we'd gotten. Jade was an easy distraction for me, and I think Chad was secretly hoping that would be the case. He and Ember clearly knew something, and I needed to focus and get us back on that track.

"We're digressing here. Chad, what the hell is going on?" I asked.

He shared one last look at Ember and sighed. "No one else can know about this. Jade's right, there are humans living amongst us here. They are mostly scientists studying us in a natural habitat."

"That's freaking creepy," I said.

"Who are they? How do they know about our kind?" Jade asked. She scooted a little closer to me on the bed and hugged my arm. Chad loved to talk when you got him started, and with Jade holding on to me like that I hoped to God he ran his mouth all night long.

"Have either of you ever heard of the Verndari?" he asked.

It sounded like something out of a sci-fi movie. I'd never heard the term before.

Jade nodded her head. "It means protector in Icelandic."

"Really?" Chad asked.

She nodded again. "I like words."

"That's kind of cool, actually," Ember said. "I mean, well, my parents are Verndari, and that's exactly how they explain it—Protectors of Shifters."

"So, they're the good guys?" I asked.

"Sort of," Chad said, going on to explain further. "The Verndari are an ancient organization. They are the descendants of Noah, I was once told. Much like God gave our kind an animal spirit to protect during the floods, Noah's people were assigned to protect us and ensure the animals roamed the Earth for all time."

"Wait, wait, wait," Jade interrupted. "If the flood wiped out all but shifters and Noah's family, doesn't that technically make all humans our protectors?"

Chad scrunched up his face in thought, then shrugged. "I guess you have a point. I don't really know how all that works, just that the Verndari were tasked to protect us, passed down from generation to generation since the days of Noah. You can usually spot them based on a specific insignia they wear." He took out his phone and showed me the picture of a ring. I was certain I'd never seen it before. "The men usually wear it as a ring, but the ladies' often come in other forms, like a broach or pendant around their neck. I've spotted a few cars adorned with it too."

"So how do you know about these Verndari?" I asked. "Through Ember's parents?"

"Actually, yes," Chad confirmed. "Her parents are Verndari. Ember's adopted."

"They didn't know what I was until I shifted for the first time. Thank God they knew though, because I don't think I could have gotten through that without them."

"Actually, there are very few Verndari who know about Ember," Chad said. "We'd like to keep it that way."

"So, are they the good guys or the bad guys then?" Jade asked the question I was most wondering too.

"Both," they said in unison.

"Those who take the sacred oaths seriously are good, but there's a new group rising that believes it's time to put the humans first and they've been known to kidnap and experiment on shifters to advance human medicines and technology. So it's a slippery slope and we don't always know for certain who to trust," Ember added.

"But they're here, watching us, and you just ignore that?" I asked. "I mean, they have to know who and what you are."

"Actually, they don't, or at least most of them don't," Chad said. "Martin's gone to great lengths to protect Ember. There's only two here that we trust absolutely and that's Dean Shannahan and Coach Meyers."

"The Athletic Director?" I asked.

They both nodded.

"But how do the others not know who you are?" I wondered aloud.

"Oh, they do," Ember assured me. "They just don't know I'm a shifter. They were told my records here were falsified. I'm a Verndari spy sent to observe only and otherwise act like a normal student." She winked and grinned.

"But you mated Chad. They have to know that," Jade blurted out. "Even I knew that, and I don't make it a habit to tune in to campus gossip."

Chad smirked. "My records were changed to show I too am not really a shifter, but of course only the Verndari know that."

"But I've seen you shift, Chad. It's been the talk of campus numerous times," I pointed out.

"Yeah, but they were only rumors as far as the Verndari know, planted to show my validity here since I transferred mid-year from a human college. If you pay attention, there's been some ridiculously wild Chad sightings recently," he said proudly. "We've been starting and spreading those ourselves even. It's kind of genius, but since Ember and I mated, that was an important cover for me in order to protect the truth about her. That's also why we got engaged so publicly and will someday have a big wedding and everything."

"So you're like double agent spies then?" Jade asked.

"Exactly. We do have to meet with Shannahan and Meyers for debriefings. The Dean is convinced we have a few Raglans placed here. We're trying to weed them out," Chad said.

"Who are the Raglans?" Jade asked.

I knew I wasn't going to like the answer and I was right.

"The Raglans are a small group of rogue Verndari. They're the bad guys, the ones I mentioned trying to experiment on our kind. If we have even one here, we need to find out who and what they're up to. So far we've come up empty; all the humans on staff appear to be Verndari, supporters of shifters."

Chad and Ember continued to fill us in with information. I was trying not to be angry that they knew all of this and had never thought to fill the rest of us in, but I also understood the chaos and panic it would cause if word of these humans watching us ever got out.

Mostly, it just fueled my need to protect Jade. I didn't give a shit about any other person on this campus. I loved my brothers, but they could fend for themselves. There was no way in hell Jade was leaving my sight anytime soon.

Jade

Chapter 19

Brett grew more and more tense the longer Chad and Ember talked. I was having trouble grasping all they were telling us, but by nature coyotes were conspiracy theorists and not very trusting. I almost laughed out loud thinking of what my mother would say if she heard this. "I told you so!"

She walked a fine line between fearing the humans and trying to pull a fast one on them claiming they were too dumb to know any better. Mostly she kept a safe distance living in small towns on large properties in the middle of nowhere and rarely staying in one place long. She kept to herself a lot with her art and gardens.

She had taught me from a young age to always trust my instincts. I hadn't second guessed they were humans. I had been certain of it, so having Chad confirm it, hadn't thrown me a curve ball, the way it appeared to be doing to Brett.

When we had exhausted the conversation and questions and Ember and I were both starting to yawn back and forth as if it was contagious, I excused myself and told them I really needed to call it a night.

It was not normal for me to be so tired at that hour. It wasn't even midnight yet, but I hadn't really slept the night before, and the stress of learning about a secret society of humans who not only knew about our kind but were actively watching us, was downright scary and weighed heavily on me.

Chad and Ember stayed in their room, but Brett got up with me. Alone in the hallway I tried to awkwardly say goodnight, but he took my hand and headed for his room. I was still too overwhelmed by everything to fight him.

When he closed his bedroom door, he immediately wrapped me up in his arms.

"Are you okay? That was, well, a lot to take in." The concern for me in his voice was evident and it crumbled the last of my resolve.

My body was shaking with emotions, not fear. I didn't think it was possible to fear anything in this man's arms.

"I'm okay," I said, honestly. "Are you?"

He pulled back just enough to look me in the eyes and shook his head. We stared at each other for a minute before he lowered his head and kissed me. It wasn't possessive or even passionate, but it definitely rocked my world like no other ever had before.

My heart raced, breaking free of the constraints I tried to keep on it. Nothing had exactly changed, other than we were aware of the real world around us now, whereas we previously had been oblivious.

Brett pulled back, resting his forehead against mine. Our mingled breaths had no rhythm and it felt like the most intimate moment I'd ever shared with anyone.

"Stay with me tonight. Please?"

He didn't have to say the words for me to know his coyote was feeling more protective over me than usual. I knew that was just the bond.

"It's not just the bond," he said.

My eyes went wide as I pulled back in shock. "Did you just hear my thoughts?" I blurted out.

Brett chuckled. "No. I don't need to hear your thoughts to know what's going through that pretty little head of yours. This isn't about my coyote or our bond, Jade. The one thing I realized tonight as Chad just turned my world upside down is that as long as you're okay, as long as you're safe, nothing else matters to me. I don't care if there's some humans watching us. They can watch all they want, but if they touch even one hair on your head, I'll kill them."

I should have been disturbed by the intensity in his voice, but instead it was a complete turn on. I'd never felt so safe and desired in my entire life. I started to tell him as much, but he cut me off with more.

"Yeah, my coyote is on edge and I'm going to probably hover for a while until that settles, but I'll sleep in the hallway outside your dorm if I have to and try to give you a little space if that's what you want. I'm asking you to stay because I want you here, but I want you to want to be here just as much."

"This afternoon I was ready to tell you that I think it would be best if we didn't see each other. I applied to a few graduate schools as far away from the ARC as possible, planning to break our bond. It was a gut reaction because I was disappointed you didn't show last night. That wasn't your fault. You didn't even know I'd be there. That was just my own insecurity. I have trouble trusting people. Maybe it's a coyote thing, maybe it's just a Jade thing. I don't know. But you have to admit Brett, you and I just don't make sense."

I could see the pain I was causing him, but I was trying to be honest. I put my finger up to his lips when he tried to speak. I wasn't done talking.

"I'm not used to all this, Brett. I'm not used to feeling so much. It's more than a little overwhelming. I'm just trying to be honest. I also know I was wrong to react so crazily. I don't want to go anywhere. Even with the threat of humans here, the ARC is my home. I'm not usually this unstable, I promise."

He smiled and relaxed just a little. "I can handle crazy, Jade. I can handle a lot of things. What I can't handle is you breaking our bond."

"What?" I asked, surprised. "I thought you'd be happy about that part. I'm the freak, remember?"

He scowled. "I called you that once."

My jaw dropped in shock. I expected to feel a punch of rejection, but it didn't come, so I decided to tease him instead. I lightly smacked his chest. "You actually called me a freak?"

He stumbled over his words as he tried to explain. "I was just mad that you were trying to screw with my family. It was before we ever met. I didn't even know you. I never should have said it. Who told you anyway?"

I started laughing. "Would you relax. No one told me, Brett. I was joking. I'm not oblivious to the nickname. Actually, I've always tried to own up to it. It really doesn't bother me. I have half a dozen shirts proclaiming it as fact."

He stared at me with a stone face I couldn't read. "You let me just stammer on for nothing?"

I grinned and rose to my tippy toes to give him a quick kiss. "Pretty much."

"Are you really going to break the bond?" he asked again, completely blindsiding me with the one-eighty in conversation.

"Is that what you want?" I asked, deflecting the question.

"No," he said without hesitation. "That's not what I want at all."

"We're so different, Brett, I mean look at us," I weakly protested.

He escorted me over to his dresser to stand before the mirror that hung on the wall above it. I was a good head shorter than him, but with my hair pulled back in a ponytail and my face clear of makeup, we really didn't look that odd.

I shook my head. "This isn't me, and you know it."

"This is you, Jade. This is you without any of your barriers up, with nothing to hide behind. I like this version, but I really like the feisty little rebel with an attitude look better." He grinned back at me in the mirror as I elbowed him. "I'm serious, Jade. We aren't nearly as different as you think."

I snorted. "Really? Explain then, because this should be good. I mean look at us."

He shrugged. "All I see is two smoking hot coyote shifters."

Before I could argue that, he brushed my ponytail to the side and began trailing kisses down my neck. It was a distraction, but there was a reason I was going to be a lawyer. I got a thrill from arguing.

"But you don't even know me. Looks aren't everything," I grumbled even while moaning as his mouth teased a particularly sensitive spot just below my ear.

He smiled against my neck and when he spoke, his breath made me shiver as my arousal for him grew.

"We've spent nearly every night together since we met, staying up late talking about absolutely everything. I know more about you than I've ever taken the time to know about anyone else. I know you argue when you're nervous, and you argue when you're happy, because you just love to argue, and I can live with that. You're going to be a phenomenal lawyer. God help the opposition that has to face you down in a courtroom. We've messed around enough that I know this spot right here," he leaned down and nibbled at that same spot again and I fought to hold back a moan, "drives you absolutely crazy, and you have a perfect little key tattoo hidden just below your left breast." He moved one of his hands up my body and rubbed the spot with his thumb before cupping at my boob as he began to toy with my nipple. I didn't know he had noticed it. It was just at the base of my heart. He looked up and stared at me in the mirror. "I know you Jade."

I was consumed with emotions and my body felt like it was on fire. I could envision the string pulling us closer together. My barriers shot up fast as I stumbled to put some space between us. I was too vulnerable with Brett. His words were beautiful, but I didn't trust he wasn't going to hurt me still.

His brow crinkled in frustration. "What just happened, Jade?"

I looked up at him and knew I couldn't lie to him or sugarcoat any of it. This was too important. "I don't want to get hurt again," my head dropped as I told him honestly. "This thing with you, it's too intense. It makes me feel too exposed."

Brett growled and my head snapped back up as my eyes went wide. "No one will ever hurt you again. You are mine. I will protect you with my life Jade. I was created for you, that's what this bond stuff is all about. Maybe we had a bit of a rocky start, but every solid mated pair I know did too. I was talking to my friend Chase about it yesterday when he called after hearing I'd found you. That's actually the real reason I didn't make it out to the lake last night. We were on the phone till almost two as he helped me sort things out. He says it'll get easier and the intensity ebbs some after our bond is sealed."

"You talked to someone about us?" I asked.

"This is all new and overwhelming to me too, so yeah. I know this can be scary, but I'm here, Jade, and I'm not going anywhere. You can count on me."

I rolled my eyes. "If it were anyone else, I'd probably laugh in your face, but I do know you. You're like freaking Captain America. Everyone on this campus loves you. Do you realize that? And you're a coyote. I don't get it."

He shrugged. "You embrace our stereotypes and just live life as yourself. I guess in some ways, I'm the true rebel because I refused to accept that and go out of my way to befriend everyone."

I sighed. "I guess in some ways you really are all-inclusive then."

He laughed. "And I'll see to it that Greek Row is too, as long as you're still willing to compromise."

"I am, but I'm not a hundred percent sure the administration will let me. Did you notice how they seemed to purposefully try to play us against each other?"

"Yeah, I noticed. After all that shit Chad told us, I'm guessing it's part of one of their experiments." I could feel Brett starting to shake and knew that everything had gotten to him more than he was going to let on.

I reached under his shirt and splayed my hands across his chest. I couldn't help but do a little research on shifter mating after discovering I had one. Skin to skin contact was supposed to help soothe and calm when your mate was experiencing heightened emotions from the bond.

The second my hands touched his heated skin, it radiated through my body. The book I'd been reading hadn't mentioned my reaction from such an act. Brett must have been either sensing my response, or calm and soothing was not the affect he was experiencing after all.

He cupped my face in his large hands and leaned his forehead against mine. The intimacy of the moment made me shudder.

"Jade, I know you're scared and overwhelmed. I hope you know I'm here and that I'm not going anywhere. I never really understood how my friends had fallen so quickly for their mates. All the crap they went through for a girl didn't really make sense to me, but I get it now, because there's nothing I wouldn't do for you. And just so we're clear, I'll wait as long as you need, but I very much want to seal this bond and spend my life with you."

I sucked in a deep breath. Things were moving so fast, but after the initial shock set in, I realized I wasn't scared or even nervous about the thought of sealing my life with Brett's. Perhaps that lack of fear terrified me even more.

I had always been one to move slowly and over examine everything in my life. I was cautious and thorough, but I knew Brett far better than I wanted to admit. Our late-night talks had opened my eyes to who he really was, and I liked that guy. He made me laugh and even relax. We weren't as fundamentally different as I tried to claim we were. Plus, he was a great kisser, amongst other things. We hadn't had sex yet, but we'd fooled around in just about every other way possible. I knew we were one hundred percent compatible. Perfect.

"I've always proceeded with caution in all areas of my life. Not this time." I stood back, breaking that bubble of intimacy and hating the look of rejection that immediately creased his face. I pulled my ponytail to the side, fully exposing my neck to him. His eyes widened in recognition and an adorable grin spread across his face. The last barriers surrounding my heart finally broke, as I willingly offered myself to him, no longer fighting the bond but leaving myself more exposed than I'd ever been before.

Brett

Chapter 20

I stood there staring at Jade. Did she really just offer herself up to me? Was she ready for that step? Was I? I hesitated for only a moment. My canines descended and I grinned at her. Flames of desire danced in her eyes and she didn't make a move to hide her neck for me.

I slowly closed the gap between us and leaned down to kiss her neck. "Mine," I whispered before sinking my teeth into the ivory column. Jade gasped, then moaned as I sucked. Her tongue lashed out and licked a spot on my neck. It made my entire body shake. I could feel her smile against my skin as I felt the sting of her teeth piercing my neck.

Desire consumed me and I couldn't undress her fast enough, but I wasn't ready to break the perfect connection as we sealed out souls together for all eternity. As I shoved her pants down, she fumbled with the button on mine. Every brush of her skin against mine was magnified by our bond.

With her lower half exposed, I quickly removed my own pants. I grabbed her by the ass and lifted her higher, as her legs easily wrapped around me. She took another long suck on my neck as I thrust into her not even stopping to grab a condom. I had never had sex without protection before. It was worth it with Jade. For that one perfect moment we were fully connected, body and soul.

As she started to grind against me, I had to pull back. Moaning, my teeth rescinded, and I gasped for air. She slowly followed. When her tongue darted out to lick a drop of blood off my new mark, it took every ounce of self-control I could muster not to prove to her I really was just a two-pump chump.

My every instinct had me walking towards the bed ready to throw her down and claim her in every way possible. While I knew Jade would love that, I also knew she needed to maintain some control, so I surprised us both turning when I hit the bed and lowering us both down so that she remained on top. I stopped kissing her long enough to dispose of her shirt and bra as I laid back to take in the view.

Her eyes were glassed over and I committed to memory the look of sheer ecstasy on her face as she settled over me and found a groove that guaranteed I wasn't going to last long. Sweat dripped across my brow as I fought not to give in to the release my body wanted so desperately.

As she changed positions just enough for me to dive even deeper into her, she started chanting my name, and I feared I was a goner. I started playing with every erogenous spot I had learned of from our previous make out sessions, trying to speed up her orgasm.

My balls were so tight it was on the cusp of being painful, but I was determined not to blow first. I had always had a problem with needing to please everyone around me, but it paled in my current obsession to please Jade.

As she rode me faster and harder, throwing her head back in pleasure, I knew I wasn't going to hold on much longer.

She yelped as I abruptly moved us, so she now lay under me. I kissed her hard on the mouth, then forced myself to become gentler. I started kissing my way down her neck and heading for her chest as I maintained the vigorous pace she had set for us.

One swipe of my tongue over her taut nipple and she fell apart in my arms. I swore her name through gritted teeth as I finally let myself go, unable to hold it back any longer. I saw stars in my vision I released so hard.

It took me a few minutes to regain any sense of control. I rolled to my back, pulling her with me. Her chest heaved against mine and I could feel her pulse racing. I grinned. I loved knowing I had that effect on her.

"Holy shit," she swore between pants as she tried to regain control of her breathing.

Holy shit was right, I thought. If I had known sex with Jade would be like that, I'd have followed her off the stage and taken her the second I knew she was my mate. I was certain there was a perma-grin setting in on my face. I'd hear shit about it later. We hadn't exactly tried to be quiet about it, but I didn't care.

As we laid there and our heartbeats began to slow, Jade's stomach growled loudly.

"Sorry." She giggled when it happened again.

"I guess we did work up an appetite," I said proudly, kissing the top of her head.

"I skipped dinner to make the meeting. Actually, I haven't eaten at all today," she confessed.

"What? Are you serious?" I asked, rolling her off of me and standing on legs that were still a little shaky as I walked to my dresser and pulled out a pair of gym shorts to throw on.

"Where are you going?" she asked with a little panic in her voice.

"Relax. I'll be right back. I'm just going to the kitchen to get you something to eat."

When I walked into the main living room, the guys hanging out in there stopped playing and talking and started clapping and cheering for me. I couldn't help myself, I grinned and bowed as I headed for the kitchen.

Should have known it wasn't going to be that easy.

"Damn, Brett. That was hot," Neal said, and everyone turned to glare at him. Jackson reached over and smacked him upside the head, and I growled before I could stop myself. "What?" he asked. Sometimes Neal could be super insightful, but most of the time he was just a complete idiot.

"So, are you official now?" Jackson asked.

I proudly turned my head to the side to show off my bond mark.

Jackson nodded. "Congratulations, man."

"Thanks."

"You're happy about this?" Reid asked.

"Of course I am." He shrugged and turned back to play video games. I knew Reid wasn't thrilled with Jade, but he'd come around.

The front door burst open and Damon came running in. "Jackson called and I came right over," he said breathlessly.

"For what?" I asked.

"A gift, for our newly fallen brother," he said, holding out his hand to pass me a dampener. The guys all started laughing like it was some joke, but I would gladly take that thing. I'd never had one myself, but I was very familiar with them.

"Thanks, dude. This is perfect," I said sincerely.

Damon hugged me. "Chad and I are here for you if you need to talk. These guys will understand someday, but I'd advise not taking advice from the unmated where Jade's concerned."

I laughed. "Dually noted."

"What are you doing out here anyway?" Jackson asked.

"Oh, food. Jade didn't eat today."

I hadn't noticed Karis walk in with Damon until she spoke up. "I'm on it. Go set that thing up and take care of your mate. I'll whip something up and bring it to you in a few minutes."

I smiled and gave her a quick hug. "Thanks Karis. You're the best."

"You da man, Brett!" Lachlan shouted as I jogged the short distance back to my room.

Jade had my pillow over her face, still lying in bed.

"Are you okay?" I asked hesitantly.

"They heard everything?" she whispered.

I laughed and shrugged. "Who cares. And it's the last they'll hear too. Damon brought us a gift." I held up the small device for her to see before plugging it in on the power strip on my desk.

"What is that?" she asked.

"It's a dampener. The upper echelon of the wolves have them. I think of it as a little magical bubble. Basically no one will hear anything that we say from outside this room."

"That's what Chad was talking about when he dragged us into his room to discuss, well, you know."

"Yup. He used to room with Chase Westin, but then he mated and bought a house just a couple of miles off campus. Chase left the dampener here not needing it at his new place. Then Damon moved in with Chad, a long story for another time, and then he met Karis. They actually live out at Chase's place now, so Damon left it behind for Chad, since they apparently have a few of them out at the cabin, too."

"Cabin? Oh, I thought maybe you were talking about the house Kaitlyn took me to that Karis and Ember were both at. It wasn't a cabin though, it was more like a small mansion but deep in the woods. Nice place."

I chuckled. "Yeah, that's the cabin. Kind of an ongoing joke. Chase told us he bought a cabin in the woods for him and Jenna, but only a Westin would consider that place a cabin. Maybe a chalet."

Jade removed the pillow from her face and sat up. Her brow furrowed as she looked around. "I thought you were bringing food."

"Karis is cooking. She'll deliver it when it's ready. I was given strict orders to get back in here and take care of my mate."

Jade laughed. "Okay, so Karis is growing on me." She covered her face with her hands and her body blushed all over. "I can't believe they heard everything. I wasn't exactly quiet."

I sat on the bed next to her and pried her hands away from her face. "I hope you never hold back just because someone might hear."

The moment quickly became surreal.

"I can't believe we actually did it," Jade said. "I mean just this morning I was convinced the best thing for us both was to split up. I don't even know at what point today that plan changed."

It hurt to hear her say that, but not as bad as it would have before I bit her. I smirked at the thought. "I'm glad it does, cause now you're stuck with me for good."

She put her arms around my neck and gave me a quick kiss. "I suppose I can live with that," she said rolling her eyes.

A knock on the door interrupted us. I jumped up and got a t-shirt and pair of sweatpants out of my drawer and threw them at her.

She rolled her eyes at me. "Seriously? I could just climb under the blanket." I yipped, startling her. Then she burst out laughing. "Okay, okay!"

There was a second knock, but I waited until Jade was fully dressed before I opened the door. When she stood up, she had to grab the pants to keep them from falling. She pulled the drawstring as tight as she could and secured them.

"Good enough?" she asked.

I nodded and opened the door.

"Whew, he's still dressed. We couldn't have interrupted too much," Damon said.

"Shut up," I grumbled.

The tray Karis was carrying was piled high with food. My mouth watered at its smell. I held the door open wide inviting her inside.

"Oh my gosh, that smells amazing!" Jade squealed in delight. "You shouldn't have, but I'm starving, so I'm glad you did."

Karis set the tray down on my desk and hugged Jade. They looked like old friends. I wasn't sure when that had happened. To the best of my knowledge they'd only met once, but it warmed my heart to see them so friendly with each other.

Damon hung back in the hallway, but when I looked up, he smiled and nodded. I knew he was trying to give Jade some space and not spook her, but I could tell he was happy for me, too.

Karis was checking out Jade's new bond mark as they giggled and shared stories. I'd never seen my mate like that before. I mean, as far as I knew, Kaitlyn was the only real friend she really had.

As Chad and Ember joined the party, I began to wonder if that was true at all. Ember squealed and threw her arms around Jade.

"I'm so happy for you," she gushed.

It felt like a party was breaking out in my room and I didn't know how to stop it.

Jade

Chapter 21

Karis and Ember seemed genuinely happy for me. I felt like I was suddenly inducted into some secret society of mated females. A part of me felt a little guilty too. If we were going to celebrate, Kaitlyn should be here too.

"I'm sorry, Jade. I know you and Brett probably want some alone time, but I couldn't help it. If everyone is going to hang out in here anyways, I had to call Kaitlyn," Ember confessed.

I had to fight back tears. "Thank you," I managed. I had never been a part of anything before and looking around I realized I not only knew these people, but they were welcoming me into their group. Brett looked relaxed and confident as he joked with his brothers.

Jackson and Lachlan had joined us too, and the room was getting a little cramped. I saw Karis shoot a sad look at the door and noticed for the first time that Damon was standing out in the hallway trying to be a part of it for Brett, while clearly giving me my space. I really appreciated that, but I also knew that I'd just signed a lifetime commitment and Damon was important to Brett.

"Excuse me a minute," I said to Ember and Karis as I left them talking and walked out into the hallway.

Damon startled when he saw me. "Sorry, I'll just. . ." he pointed back to the common room and started to turn to leave.

"Don't go," I said.

He stared at me in surprise. "Really?"

I shrugged. "I like Karis, and she says you're not that guy I met freshman year. I can see that. Plus, you're important to Brett, and he's kind of important to me. I can't believe I'm actually saying this, but I forgive you if you can forgive me." I sighed, waiting for his reaction.

"What do I need to forgive you for?" he asked with a smirk.

I rolled my eyes. "I haven't exactly been nice to you, and a small part of being vocal about campus inclusion has been about revenge for freshman year, well, you know. I was humiliated and wanted all the D.O.G.s to pay for that. I was wrong. That's not a word I'm very familiar with and it leaves a terrible taste in my mouth, so please don't make me say it again."

He laughed and I saw some of the tension release from his shoulders. I felt a little guilty that I was likely the cause of that tension being there to begin with.

"Besides," I added. "I've never really had a lot of friends, but since meeting Kaitlyn this year, I realize I don't hate people as much as I thought I did." I smiled. "And I really like Karis and don't want things to be awkward every time we're all around each other. Plus, like I said earlier, you're important to Brett, and he's important to me." I shrugged and offered him my hand. "Fresh start?"

Damon genuinely smiled and shook my hand. "Damon Rossi, it's nice to meet you."

I laughed remembering how Brett had done the same thing after our take two kiss. I rolled my eyes and shook my head. "Jade Michaels. It's nice to meet you."

I turned to head back into the room and noticed Brett standing in the doorway watching us. Damon walked around me and hugged him.

"Congrats man," I heard him say, though Brett was still staring at me with a look of gratitude on his face that was making me feel a little exposed and awkward.

Before things could get weird, Kaitlyn ran in and practically tackled me in the hallway.

"I can't believe you sealed your bond so quickly. That's crazy, girl. But I'm so proud of you and so happy for the both of you."

Brett stepped out to join us, and Kaitlyn threw an arm around him to pull us both into a group hug. The second Brett's hand hit my lower back, my whole body lit on fire. I fought not to blush. It embarrassed me how responsive I was to him. I glanced over at him and knew from the sparkle in his eye that he was very aware of my reaction too.

When Kaitlyn finally let us go, Brett wrapped me up fully in his arms and kissed my forehead. "Sorry about all this," he apologized.

"It's okay," I said, and I truly meant it.

"Did you really make amends with Damon?"

I smiled up at him and nodded. "It needed to be done. I know he's your friend, and I really do like Karis."

"Thank you," he said, hugging me tightly until the guys started to comment, and then Brett left me to go back into his room.

I remained in the hallway with Kaitlyn.

"Are you happy, Jade?" she asked.

I smiled at my friend. "Actually, I am. I mean it's insane. Right? We haven't even known each other a week yet, but I know him, Kaitlyn. I can't even describe it. I think when you know, you just know. No regrets, no doubts. But ask me again tomorrow when the buzz of it wears off, and I may tell you a different story," I teased.

It didn't take long for Karis and Ember to join us as the guys talked in the room. We made plans to all have dinner together the next week. Everything seemed to be falling into place.

It took another hour before Brett's room finally cleared and we were alone again.

"I should probably go. It's getting late, even by our standards," I commented.

Brett frowned and shook his head. "Stay." It wasn't a demand, more like a plea. I really didn't want to leave him either.

"I shouldn't. I don't exactly want to do the walk of shame across campus in the morning," I groaned.

"Stay," he insisted, and I didn't have the heart to resist him.

"Fine. I'll stay for a few hours at least," I said, rolling my eyes. In truth I had never felt so wanted in my entire life, and it felt so good I really didn't want to leave.

We didn't have sex again, we just talked for a bit, and then fell asleep wrapped up in each other's arms.

It was still dark when I walked across campus to my dorm, alone as usual. I felt a sting in my neck just before the world began to fade around me as I collapsed to the cold, hard ground.

I awoke with a pounding headache. My mouth was dry, and I was shivering. There was a constant hum in the air like the sound of machinery. It seemed odd, so I slowly opened my eyes.

My heart began to race when I saw the bars surrounding me and I sat up too quickly, banging my head on the hard steel above. I was naked and alone in a cage. The room was brightly lit and freezing. I couldn't stop my hands from shaking as I reached out and grasped the cold bars.

"Hello?" I yelled out to the room. "Is anyone there?"

My cries were met with absolute silence. I backed myself into the far corner and examined my situation. Lights flooded the room, but there didn't appear to be any windows. I stuck my hand out behind me and touched the wall. It was concrete and cold. There was a high probability I was underground. A basement maybe? Was I even still at the ARC? Where was Brett?

I was flooded with questions, but aside from the humming sound of machines, I couldn't hear anything to help me discern where I was or who had taken me. I tried to slow my heartrate as well as my breathing. I was on the verge of hyperventilating, and I was shaking all over. I had never been so scared in all my life, but that wasn't going to help me get out of here.

I needed to calm down and think rationally. I was good at tamping down my emotions to calculate situations. Well, I was, before Brett.

Brett. Where was he? He didn't even know I'd left. I'd never said goodbye. Was he still safe in his room at the doghouse? How long would it take for him to notice I was gone? Would he even care? Maybe he would be relieved. Before tonight I'd never really had any friends. Had that really changed? Would anyone come looking for me? Would anyone care?

Doubt seeped in, leaving me feeling more alone than I'd ever felt before. I pulled my knees to my chest and let myself have a few moments to wallow in self-pity, then I realized that wasn't going to get me out of this nightmare. Pushing down those feelings of insecurity I tried to assess my situation.

The box I was sitting in was solid on the top, bottom, and both sides. The front and back were barred, but the back was against the concrete wall, leaving only one entry or exit point.

I scooted forward and checked the bars for a lock or some sort of way to open. I couldn't find anything. I grabbed hold of the bars and jerked them as hard as I could. They weren't going anywhere.

Pressing my face up against the bars I tried to get a better view of the room layout. It was obvious I was up high. To either side and below me it appeared to be nothing but bars, perhaps additional cages like mine.

"Hello? Is anyone here?" I yelled out again. "Hello? Can anyone hear me?" I grabbed and pushed and pulled against the bars again. "Hello?" I screamed.

"Keep it down up there, we're trying to sleep," someone finally yelled.

"She must be new here," another voice said.

"Yeah, saw them bring her in last night. Didn't look like the kind anyone would be missing. She ain't gonna help us get out of here, so go back to sleep already," the first voice said.

I wasn't alone, yet I felt even more isolated than before. I knew these guys wouldn't help me get out of here either, but I needed whatever information they knew.

"Where are we?" I asked. "Please. Why am I here?"

"You're nothing more than a lab rat to these guys. Keep your head down and stay quiet. The accommodations may suck, but they feed us well and only require a little blood each day. It's the ones that ask too many questions and make too much noise that end up on the table," a new voice that sounded much closer replied.

"The table?" I asked.

I saw a hand reach out between the bars to my left and point. I looked in that direction and noticed a metal table in the middle of the room. There was a white sheet covering it and it appeared to have a body under it.

My hands flew to my mouth as I bit back a scream. My eyes darted around the room. There was lab equipment everywhere. That must be the humming sound that was driving me insane. There were also two more metal tables with IV poles next to them along with other medical equipment.

The experiments. Chad had said the Raglans were experimenting on shifters. I had to get out of there. I couldn't die here. My vision darkened around the edges as I began to breathe too fast. I tried to gulp in air to wave it off, but everything went black as I fainted.

When I started to come to again, I stretched out and quickly realized I was no longer trapped. I felt sick to my stomach and grabbed the blanket to pull it tighter around me. *It was only a dream*, I began chanting to myself.

"She's awake," an all-too-familiar voice said, making the hairs on the back of my neck stand up.

"You gave her the shot, right? There's no way she can shift?" a woman asked.

"No way," the man confirmed. "Wake up, Jade."

My eyes shot open as I saw Professor Rodgers standing over me with a malicious smile and a bone saw in his hand. He fired it up and laughed.

I shot up quickly and hit my head hard. Against what? I didn't know. I just knew I was in danger. I screamed and screamed, thrashing out to deter him as best I could.

Brett

Chapter 22

"Wake up, Jade," I said. It was clear she was having some sort of nightmare. Without warning, she shot up and our heads collided hard. Mine was throbbing, but she seemed unaffected as she started lashing out, kicking and punching in all directions.

I started to panic and shake her when she let out a blood curdling scream.

"Jade, wake up. Wake up, baby. It's just a nightmare!" I was trying to restrain her before she hurt herself more. My head was already pounding.

I somehow managed to get my hands on her arms and began to shake her.

"Jade, please, wake up," I begged.

Her eyes shot open and the fear I saw there chilled me to the bone. My coyote immediately went on high alert trying to identify the threat, but there was none. It was only a nightmare.

"You're safe, Jade. I'm here. You're safe," I said as I tried to pull her to my chest, sensing the worst was over. "It was just a dream. Just a really bad dream," I reassured her as I rubbed her back and held her close.

She was shaking violently in my arms and her nails pierced my skin as she tried to hold on for dear life. I didn't mind. The temporary pain was nothing compared to what she'd obviously been experiencing.

"Brett?" she whispered in a hoarse voice. "Is it really you?"

"I'm here. This is real. You just had a nightmare."

She looked up at me, a little of the confusion still clouding her beautiful green eyes began to clear just before they filled with tears. She wrapped her arms around me and cried into my chest until there were no more tears left to shed.

"I'm so-sorry," she stuttered. "It just felt so real."

"Do you want to talk about it?" I asked and she shook her head, refusing to even look at me. I had thought Jade was vulnerable a few times in our short time together, but I just realized I'd never truly seen her vulnerable until now. Whatever it was that haunted her so badly, I would do anything to obliterate it permanently. "I won't push you, but my mom always said it helps to talk about stuff like that. She says that opening up and sharing your nightmares is the only way to keep them from coming back. I'm a good listener if you change your mind."

She sighed, starting to finally calm a little. Sitting back, she sniffled and wiped at her puffy eyes.

"It's kind of stupid now, I guess. I think everything we learned yesterday about the Verndari and the Raglan just got to me more than I thought."

I tensed. What Chad had shared with us hadn't set well with me either. Something needed to be done to stop them, I just didn't know what. If these human intruders were scaring Jade this badly, I had to find a way to rid our campus of them.

"What's your schedule like today?" I asked her.

"My classes start at one. I have about a two-hour break for dinner and then I'm in class until nine," she said.

"On a Friday night?" I asked, unsure she realized what day it was.

Jade shrugged. I knew she was still shaken from her nightmare, and there was no way I was going to just leave her all day, so I needed to know what schedule I was working around.

"I never really thought of it. I prefer later classes, cause well, you know why. I've never really had any reason why Friday night would be much different. Half the time my last class gets cancelled anyway."

"But not tonight?" I asked.

She shrugged. "I'll have to check online. I don't usually know for sure until around noon, sometimes later even. He usually sends out a class text."

I was trying to piece her schedule together with my own when her phone dinged signaling an incoming text. I smiled, optimistically and handed it to her. The second she looked at the screen, I knew it wasn't the news I was hoping for. Jade's face turned ashen and she started to shake again.

"What is it?" I asked, trying to maintain a calm exterior even though she was likely already a terrified wreck.

"Rodgers wants to have lunch to discuss the details for the battle," she whispered.

"Where?" I asked.

"In his office."

"Not happening. Move it to the café so we can keep an eye on you. If he's serious about it, he'll agree to it, though I really don't know why he would want to when we both know he's lying."

"I know. A part of me wants to go just to see what he says, but, um, in my dream, it was his face I saw there," she said looking like she'd just seen a ghost.

"Saw where?" I asked.

She shrugged. "It was a lab of some sort. They kept all the shifters in cages like animals and experimented on them in front of us. I was on the table when you woke me up and it was Professor Rodgers about to experiment on me. It was so real, Brett. I just don't know if I'm ready to face him. I'm not sure I can differentiate what's real and what's not, even knowing it was just a dream. It was that vivid."

I wasn't used to feeling angry, but I was ready to punch someone. Unfortunately for Chad, he chose that moment to knock on our door. I got up to answer it and unleashed my temper on him.

One moment he was standing before me, the next I had him pinned up against the wall across the hallway yelling.

"You scared the shit out of her man! Why did you have to tell us that crap?"

Jade was at my side instantly, and when she put her hands on my arms all the fight left me and I dropped Chad to the ground.

"I don't know what you're talking about, man," Chad said.

I instantly felt bad. "I know. I'm sorry. I just don't know what to do or how to handle everything we learned yesterday. Jade's having nightmares from it, now Rodgers wants to meet her for lunch. How the hell do you handle this shit?"

I offered him my hand and pulled him up off the floor. Chad looked around and shuffled us back into my room, closing the door before he spoke.

"Be careful with Rodgers. Ember and I have been watching him very closely. I'm not trying to scare you, I'm just being honest. I know it's a lot to take in. Trust me, I know. I wish you guys hadn't stumbled into this mess. Walking around oblivious to all of this is so much easier," Chad confessed.

"No. We need to know. We need to be diligent. Why Rodgers?" Jade asked.

I was wondering the same thing.

Chad sat down at my desk and Jade and I took the bed.

"Rodgers has been disappearing a lot lately, cancelling classes and stuff. We've tried to follow him, but he always seems to just disappear somewhere in the vicinity of the science department. Ember and I have searched and searched, but we can't seem to figure out where he's going."

"If it's a hidden lab in the basement, I'm going to puke," Jade said.

"Was that from your dream?" I asked, taking her hand and giving it a squeeze of reassurance.

She nodded. "Yes, and I know it was all fabricated by my imagination, but it just felt so damn real. I can't shake it."

"That's really not out of the realm of possibilities," Chad said. I shot him a look that said *Shut up!*

He clearly didn't get it. "Tell me what you saw."

Jade looked at me and I shrugged.

"Does it matter? I mean it was all made up," Jade said. I was thinking the same thing.

"Maybe. I'm just grasping at straws here really."

"You don't have to." I told Jade.

"It's fine. Maybe talking about it will help put it out of my mind. I mean it was so real. Terrifying really. In my dream, I was tranquilized walking back to my dorm. I didn't see anyone, I just felt the sting of the dart and everything went black. I woke up in a cage. It was solid steel on the floor, the ceiling, and both sides so I couldn't see who was in the cage next to me. The front and back were barred, though I could feel a cold concrete wall behind me and assumed I was in a basement. I wasn't the only shifter there, and cages were stacked all along the wall, one on top of the other like some kind of high-tech kennel."

I shuddered as she talked. "You don't have to do this," I reminded her.

"No, go on, please," Chad insisted.

Jade nodded. "There was a constant humming like the low noise made from a computer or something, but it was louder and drove me insane. And there were other shifters there, but I could only hear them. I never actually saw any of them. At some point I blacked out and when I woke up again, I was on one of the lab tables. There were four of them in the middle of the room. There was medical equipment and stuff all around and Rodgers was standing over me with a bone saw. That's when I started screaming and Brett woke me up."

I rubbed her lower back as she finished her story, and then melted into my side. Chad sat there quietly. Then he got up and began pacing the room.

"Was that bone saw a large one—like a, 'hack-off-a-limb' saw, or a small one, more like a Dremel tool?" Chad asked.

"Dude, it was a dream," I said.

"More like a Dremel tool," Jade said, her curiosity clearly getting the best of her.

Chad stopped pacing and approached us slowly. "May I?" he asked before touching my mate.

Jade shrugged, then nodded. Chad carefully pulled her back. He was clearly looking for something, but I wasn't sure what. I didn't like him so close to my bond mark, or that his hands were on my mate. The only thing keeping me from lashing out at him again was the fact that I knew he was happily mated.

He turned her head to the other side and continued his search in her hairline. I saw it at the same time he did, a distinctive scar behind her left ear hidden under her hair.

"What is that?" I asked.

"Holy shit! The Raglan are here," Chad proclaimed.

My stomach churned uneasily. "Babe, have you ever had stitches back here?"

"No," she said. "What are you talking about?"

"Think hard, Jade. Have you ever cut yourself or bumped your head hard enough to require stitches? Ever? Even as a child?" I asked, needing to believe anything but what Chad was insinuating.

"No. I can call my mother to be certain, but not that I know of."

Her answer chilled me to the bone. I met Chad's stare. His eyes were wild and a little glazed over. It only took a few minutes for Ember to burst through the door, slamming it behind her.

"You're certain?" she asked.

"It can't be more than a few months old, Em," he said. "Come here and see for yourself."

Jade stirred. "What the hell is it? I'm sort of freaking out down here."

I rubbed her back a little more aggressively, more from my own agitation than for her comfort. "You have a scar, Jade. Chad thinks it was fairly recent."

"Her description of the lab was way too close to the last few we shut down. I don't think that was just a dream she had, Brett."

"What?" Jade screeched.

Ember sat down on the opposite side of Jade and gave her a hug. "If this is what we suspect, they've already gotten to you, Jade. You've been experimented on. It's not the first time we've seen this happen. They use memory suppression drugs, so you don't remember anything, but all the drugs really do is repress your memories. Learning the truth yesterday must have stirred them up. You probably can't remember if you tried, but your dreams tap into different parts of the brain. I think you were reliving what happened to you."

Jade

Chapter 23

I sat there quietly wracking my brain to make any sense at all of what Chad and Ember were saying. Was there any possible validity to this? Had I been kidnapped and held in that awful place without realizing it?

I thought hard as they stared at me in concern. Two months ago, I'd gotten sick with the flu shortly after settling back in on campus after summer break. I remembered going for a late-night run. That wasn't uncommon for me, but I woke up in the wee hours of the morning in my bed with a terrible flu. My head had pounded for days and I'd stayed in my dorm, in and out of consciousness as I tried to sleep it off. I remembered later because it was very rare for a shifter to get sick like that, and the more I thought about it, the more I realized that I couldn't remember anything from my run in the woods, until I woke up sick in my bed.

Once I'd gone through the worst of it and was feeling better, I had been shocked to realize five days had passed. It hadn't felt like that long, but it would make sense if they'd tried to erase my memories of that awful place.

I started to retch at the thought. Brett grabbed a trashcan next to his desk and held it under me as I vomited violently.

"Is she okay?" Chad asked.

"I suspect she's just remembering," Ember said sadly. "I have to call my dad. If the Raglan have taken to experimenting on students, we have to stop them."

"I remember," I said hoarsely after I was certain I wouldn't throw up again. Brett got up for only a minute to open his mini fridge and bring me a bottle of cold water. I opened it and slowly sipped it. "Thanks," I said weakly.

"You really remember?" Chad asked.

"Sort of," I said. "It was about two months ago. I went for a run, then everything got fuzzy. I woke up in my bed sometime later sick with the flu. I remember feeling like someone took a baseball bat to the back of my head right in the area you guys are telling me I have a scar now."

"Jade, shifters don't get sick with the flu. We're naturally immune," Brett said.

"No shit, Sherlock. That's why I vividly remember it, timeline and all."

Ember hung up the phone. "Dad's flying in immediately. He recommended we all pay a visit to Dean Shannahan and fill him in."

"How can we trust him?" Brett asked.

I was thinking the same thing.

"Martin trusts him," Chad said. "We can too. He'd never put his daughter at risk."

"Sorry, but I don't know, Martin. No offence Ember," Brett said.

"None taken," she assured him.

"I only care about protecting Jade," he said.

I gave him a weak smile and scooted a little closer to my mate.

"No more going out alone at night," Chad told me. "You've said yourself you were a classic loaner with few friends. Heck, Kaitlyn claims to be your only friend."

"She's not wrong," I mumbled.

"That just made you a sitting duck. They had easy access since coyotes tend to be more nocturnal anyways, and since you had few to no friends, no one would come looking for you when you disappeared. They could have kept you for a few days even, and it was likely no one would have noticed," Chad said.

"Not anymore," Brett assured me. "And that goes for everyone. I don't want anyone from our house going out alone at night. There's safety in numbers. Until these assholes are found and addressed, we need to be on full alert."

"They aren't likely to target any of the Greeks, Brett," Ember said, trying to soothe his fears. "They're looking for easy targets, not community shifters that would definitely be noticed if we went missing."

"I don't care. I couldn't live with myself if this happened to another person I care about. We need to warn Kaitlyn too."

"We have to be careful how we phrase it though. I'm serious, Brett. You don't know the kind of riots it would stir up if word got out that there were humans at the ARC kidnapping shifters for experiments. Warn them however you must, but be discreet about it," Chad warned. "And no mention of the Verndari. We had a deal."

I could tell Brett wasn't happy, but he nodded.

Ember's phone had been blowing up with texts ever since she hung up with her dad.

"We need to get to the Dean's office. Dad already called and filled him in. He's asking to speak with you, Jade."

"Absolutely not," Brett said. I looked at him and he shook his head. "No. I don't want you near any of them."

I took his hands in mine. "Ember really believes he's one of the good guys. We have to trust her on this if we stand any hope of shutting this down. Whatever they need from us, it's okay, especially if it stops even one more shifter from going through that."

"Please, no," he practically begged.

"I'm going to be okay, Brett. Mainly because you aren't going to leave my side. We can do this, together," I told him.

He considered it for a few moments, then sighed in resignation. "Don't leave my sight or my coyote is going to go batshit crazy. Are we clear?"

I nodded my head and bit back a smile noticing Chad and Ember were nodding in agreement, too.

They left to give Brett and me privacy to change before we left. I put the clothes on that I'd worn the day before, and then groaned as I pulled on the jeans and colorful shirt. I frowned when I looked in the mirror and tried to fix my ponytail.

"Can we please stop by my dorm on the way? Dean Shannahan literally saw me in this yesterday and I feel so. . . ugh! I don't even look or feel like myself. I need my armor to get through today," I whined.

"Yes, I agree. The more normal you look, the less attention this will draw."

I laughed. "No one ever claimed that I look normal," I reminded him.

He frowned. "Normal for you. Is that better?"

I shrugged. "I know I'll feel a lot closer to normal in my regular clothes, even if I have to dig something out of the hamper."

It was his turn to laugh. "We'll do your laundry tonight. You can bring it over here if you want. It's free."

"You have a regular washer and dryer? No coin slot?"

"Yup," he said. "Best kept secret on campus."

I pointed to the back of my head. "You sure about that?"

His forehead crinkled into a full scowl.

I laughed. "Too soon?"

Without answering he pushed me towards the door. We met back up with Chad and Ember and they followed me over to my room, keeping me in sight at all times, but at a safe enough distance not to attract attention. It took some convincing, but Brett stayed outside my dorm while Ember went in with me. We agreed that would be less conspicuous.

I grabbed an outfit off the top of my hamper and gave it a quick sniff. Good enough! I went to the bathroom to change and couldn't resist jumping in the shower. I was fast, and only put the basic layer of makeup on, but once I was ready and my teeth were brushed, I felt like maybe I could survive the next few hours without a complete meltdown.

Brett whistled softly as I stepped back outside. I caught his grin of appreciation as he checked me out and blushed, even though I was pretending we weren't together.

Ember led the way ahead of me. I followed at a safe distance and Chad hung back with Brett, mostly because he was the loose cannon in the equation. Even though we were bonded, it was still very new, and his coyote was on edge knowing I had been and was potentially still in danger.

The trek across campus felt longer than it ever had before. We kept our distance from each other until we reached the Dean's house. I was surprised we went there and not his office. Of course I knew where he lived, everyone did, but I personally didn't know anyone who had ever been there. At least not that I knew of.

The way Ember walked around to the back and let herself in with an air of confidence told me that this was not an unfamiliar meeting for her.

I held back and waited for Brett and Chad to catch up before entering the house. Chad led the way as Brett and I followed, his hand possessively settled on my hip.

"Come in, all of you. Make yourselves at home. Martin should be along shortly. He phoned to say his plane was about to land. Fortunately, he only had a quick hop by jet to get here," the Dean said.

"That was fast," I commented without meaning to.

Dean Shannahan chuckled. "My dear, he was on his plane before he even got off the phone with Ember this morning. That man does not mess around when it comes to the safety of his daughter, or anyone else here at the ARC. He didn't take the time to really fill me in on what's happened. I know this has to do with. . ." he hesitated and looked to Ember before proceeding further.

"Jade discovered the truth and we confirmed it, and to impress upon her the importance of keeping it quiet," Ember said.

"And Brett? I mean, it's no big secret around campus that the two of them do not get along," he said, completely ignoring the fact we were both right there listening, and it irritated me.

I crossed my arms over my chest. "No, that's not some big secret. The biggest secret really is that he's my mate. And no, I don't hate him. We may not always agree on things, but that's okay. We're learning to work through that," I said.

The Headmaster's jaw nearly hit the floor. I wasn't sure anything would have shocked him more. The man was literally stunned silent.

"It's true, sir," Ember confirmed. "So, anything you ask or say to Jade, Brett either already knows, or he will soon enough. It's safe to talk."

"Well, um, okay. I suppose the staff can forget about their little social experiment, trying to see how far they can push the two of you before one or both of you erupt upon each other then," he confided.

"You wanted to see how much crap we could take before shifting on each other?" I asked.

"Basically, that was what they were looking for," he admitted.

I laughed. "No offense sir, but you really don't know much about shifters, do you? Sure, there are a few hot-heads who shift in frustration, but it would take a whole lot more than anything you guys could throw our way to cause that reaction, especially after I caught your scent and realized it was fake."

He frowned. "Is it really that noticeable?"

Chad shook his head. "No, it's not, but I have a hypothesis about that. Since we're fairly certain the nightmare Jade had was a repressed memory, I believe she learned of the humans during that period and caught on to the underlying scent. She didn't know the association her brain was making at the time when she thought she had just discovered it."

I looked at Brett and he shrugged. "It would make sense." He stepped forward and took a big sniff of Shannahan, shaking his head. "No, I mean maybe there's a tiny bit of the metallic smell you mentioned, but it's so faint I would never have noticed it. I think Chad's onto something."

The Dean looked relieved. "Thank you. I feel strongly that with the threat of the Raglan on campus it's more important than ever for me to be here to watch over you all."

"But you didn't," Brett said. "Jade was experimented on, treated like a lab rat under your watch," Brett said, letting go of some of his anger.

"I'm sorry," the Dean said, blanching at the thought. "I never dreamed they'd do something like this knowing we were here, and the school is protected by the Verndari. I have failed you all. When this is over and we've gotten to the bottom of this and are certain the school is safe again, if you wish for me to step down as your Headmaster, I will."

"No," Ember said. "My dad trusts very few Verndari right now with everything happening. He trusts you. We can't afford to lose that here. We all knew there was a possibility that the Raglan had infiltrated here. Chad and I have been watching for any clues to their whereabouts. None of us dreamed they'd go this far. It's not your fault."

I didn't go into details and we didn't formulate a plan until after Ember's dad finally arrived.

It was in my nature to be skeptical of people, but I liked Martin Kenston from the second he walked into the room, and I got a little starstruck when Alicia Kenston followed closely behind him.

The two of them immediately went to Ember and checked over every hair on her head until they were both convinced she was truly okay. Then they moved on to Chad and finally Brett. It amazed me how caring they both were, and it softened me towards them, seeing the way they fussed over Brett as if he were one of their own.

I stood by awkwardly and watched. When Alicia was certain Brett was okay, she turned to me. Before I knew what was happening, she had me in her arms.

"You must be Jade. You poor thing, you've been through so much. How are you holding up?" she asked.

To my horror, I lost it in this stranger's arms. Everything I'd been bottling up inside since the second I smelled the fake scent on Professor Rodgers came barreling out and I sobbed in her arms.

She quickly shooed everyone out of the room as she stood there holding me while I cried. I knew Brett was pacing nearby, upset and unsure of what to do. As the tears slowed and I started to regain control of myself, I started apologizing.

"I'm so sorry. This isn't like me at all. I don't even know why I'm crying," I said fighting back a case of the hiccups.

I could feel Brett's anger rising, and I knew it wasn't directed at me. Alicia finally let me go, and Brett wrapped me up the second I was free. I breathed in his scent and let it soothe me. He kissed the top of my head.

"Sweetheart, this isn't unusual behavior. From what Ember has told us, you were violated in the worst way imaginable. While your memories may not be clear, they are still there haunting you. Just let it out. It's okay to cry," Alicia assured me.

I nodded against Brett's chest, but I was already sobering up.

"I'm sorry," I told him. "I'm okay. I really am. I think I just needed to get that out."

He nodded but didn't say a word.

Martin walked back in to check on us. He smiled at the sight.

"Chad just told us congratulations are in order. I can't even begin to imagine everything you're going through, Jade. When you're ready, we have some questions. They won't be easy, I'm sure, but they'll help get to the bottom of things and rid this campus of these scum. I will personally see to it that they pay for what they've done to you, and who knows how many others here."

"Thank you, sir," Brett managed to say. "Just give us a couple of minutes."

"Take your time, son," Martin said.

Alicia patted my back in a show of reassurance as she passed, following her husband back into the next room where the others had gone to give me some space.

"Bet you didn't bargain for all this when you agreed to mate me," I said, trying to lighten the mood some.

His hand gently lifted my chin to tilt my head back, so that I was forced to look at him.

"Together forever, Jade. I know it may not feel like it right now, but we're going to get through this and we're going to do it together."

My heart swelled and a different kind of tears blurred my eyes as I reached up to pull him down towards me. He smiled against my lips when he kissed me.

I let that kiss linger only a moment before I pulled back.

"Okay, let's do this."

Brett

Chapter 24

It took about an hour to go over everything Jade could remember about the lab she'd been taken to. Martin had been able to confirm the scar on the back of her head, and he and Chad even discussed some possible ideas about why. Of course, no one else in the room had the knowledge to understand what the hell they were talking about.

Chad and Ember had been watching Rodgers closely and had a vague idea of which buildings we should look at. I was pressing for us to get moving faster. Jade had a noon meeting scheduled with Professor Rodgers, and I very much would prefer it if she didn't have to go. That would mean finding the lab and getting the information we needed for the good Verndari to take him down.

I couldn't understand why we were stalling. Their meeting was less than two hours away.

Most of us startled when the front door opened, but Martin and Shannahan just smiled and stood to great the newcomers. I got a sick feeling in my stomach, fearing we'd just set a trap for ourselves. I quickly examined the layout of the room, something I should have done when we first sat down and formulated an escape plan for Jade. She was my first priority. I'd worry about myself and the others when I knew she was safe.

My fears ebbed only slightly when Coach Meyers walked in. I glanced at Ember. She nodded and mouthed, "Safe," to me. But when Patrick O'Connell walked in behind him, followed by my friends, Chase and Jenna, I was finally able to relax.

Patrick was from Westin Pack. He'd visited when Chase was living in the doghouse enough for me to get to know him. He was mated to Chase's oldest sister, Elise, and was an overall cool guy. I was surprised when he greeted Martin as if they were old friends.

Chase walked straight to me and I rose to accept his hug. We had been through a lot together over the years. He was my brother through and through.

"What the hell are you doing here?" I asked.

"Martin called Patrick to fill him in on what was happening here. Jenna and I were already planning to drive up later today and surprise you. No way were we missing out on this epic open Row party you're throwing tomorrow."

I had forgotten all about the party. It felt like a distant memory after everything else that had happened in the last twenty-four hours.

"It's really great to see you, man," I said. I reached down and took Jade's hand, pulling her up from the couch she was sitting on. "Chase, this is Jade, my mate," I said proudly.

Jade rolled her eyes but smiled when she shook his hand. "I fear he's going to be telling every single person we pass today."

Jenna laughed. "Trust me, it could be worse. Hi, I'm Jenna, Chase's mate."

Jade shook hands with her, too. "It's nice to meet the both of you."

Ember and Chad rose to greet them as well. There was a time when I was a little jealous of how close the two couples were. It made me feel left out in some ways whenever I was with them. With Jade at my side, I didn't feel like that anymore.

"Okay, now that we're all here and Patrick's been updated on the plan, it's time to move out," Dean Shannahan said.

We had gone over the plan for what seemed like a hundred times already, so it was about time as far as I was concerned. The only part I truly liked about the plan was that I got to stay with Jade. Now, if we could just wrap things up before she actually had to meet that asshole, then life would be good again.

Patrick was assigned to Jade and me. For that I was grateful. I knew him better than Martin or the Headmaster. I trusted him more. Ember and Chad stayed with Martin, and Chase and Jenna joined the search with Dean Shannahan.

We said our goodbyes and headed off to our designated targets. For us, that was the science building. Jade walked around the backside of the building and shook her head.

"This isn't it." she said.

"How can you possibly know that?" I asked. "You were drugged, remember? This building has a basement. We should at least check it out."

"It is a little obvious," Patrick said, watching Jade closely. "But sometimes being in plain sight is the best option."

Jade shook her head. "I'm telling you it doesn't feel right."

She stopped and turned around slowly. I could tell she was desperately trying to remember something. Anything. I started to protest again, but Patrick held up a hand to stop me.

"Give her a minute," he said. "She's still our best lead."

"But if we spook these people, they'll ghost and we'll never get justice for what they did to Jade," I growled.

"I understand man. We missed the team that took Lily by minutes. They had to leave a lot behind, which helped, but I'm well aware of how fast they can move," he confessed.

"Lily Westin? Chase's sister?" I asked.

He nodded. "Yeah, they got her up in Alaska. Martin and I have a mutual friend that was undercover at the time and was able to alert me. Even with an inside man, we still couldn't move fast enough."

"I hadn't heard about that. She's mated to the Collier Alpha now, though, so I know you got her out safe."

"We did, and she's fine. Maybe you want to consider introducing her to Jade sometime. Lily would be a great person for her to talk with. You know, someone who's been through what she's facing now."

"Thanks, I'll see if I can arrange that."

Jade started walking away from the science building. I went to call out to her, but Patrick stopped me.

"She may not have conscious memories, but subconsciously they're still clearly there. If she has a feeling in this direction, we need to follow it," he said.

I nodded and we followed. Jade walked down the alley that ran along the backside of the science building, then turned right at a dumpster.

"Where's she going? There's nothing there," I said in a low voice.

Patrick shrugged, but Jade stopped and turned back towards us. She smiled and waved us over. I peeked behind the dumpster, but there was only a brick wall. I looked around trying to figure out what building we were at.

"It's the computer lab," Jade said. "Listen closely and you can make out the humming I was talking about, even from out here."

I listened and sure enough I could hear the low mechanical hum of computers. Not just the lab computers either. "I know this place," I said. "It's also the campus data center. That's probably why the noise sounded so loud and distinctive to you."

"Come on, we'll walk around to the front and see if we can find a way into the basement," Patrick said.

I looked the building over. "From here it doesn't look like this building even has a basement. But it's got to be close by." I strained my neck down the alleyway to try to find something we could work with.

Jade huffed. "Guys, it's here," she said.

"Where Jade? There's nothing but a brick wall here," I told her.

She moved the dumpster back a little and pointed again.

"Holy shit! Would you fecking look at that," Patrick said.

If you looked closely at the bricks, you could see they aligned in the shape of a door. The problem was, there was no doorknob. Patrick pushed against the bricks, but they didn't budge. He had us spread out and look for some sort of access control. There was none to be found.

Patrick pulled out his phone and dialed a number.

"Archie, I need you to work your magic. Don't let me down." He leaned up against the brick wall. "I need full schematics for the building at my coordinates. And if you could pull up satellite imagery for the past few weeks and find out who has been coming and going from here and how the bloody hell they're getting in, I'd really appreciate it."

He hung up and dialed another number.

"Cormack, we think we found it, but there are a few complications. We've literally run into a brick wall."

I snickered at his pun despite the severity of the situation.

"Who's Archie? And who the hell is Cormack?" I asked when he hung up.

"Archie works for me. Best mole in the world. He can crack into anything on the internet. He'll have what we need soon. And Cormack? Dude, that's your Headmaster," Patrick laughed.

"Cormack?" I shrugged. "I did not know that."

Jade looked down at her watch. "Only twenty minutes until my meeting," she said nervously. "I don't think we're going to make it."

"Give my guys a few more minutes. Archie will have something. I promise."

Another five minutes passed before his phone rang.

"Please tell me it's good news," Patrick said as he answered the phone. I could hear that someone was talking on the other end but couldn't make out what was being said. "Dammit, Arch, I said good news! Yeah, okay. Send the blueprints over so I have an idea of what I'm dealing with when we do get inside."

He hung up the phone and turned towards Jade.

"I'm sorry Jade. Looks like you're going in. Archie is pulling up facial recognition for everyone that has come in and out of this place for the last two months. This Professor Rodgers has already been confirmed. I'm going to need you to stall him for as long as possible. He has a one o'clock class, so if you can use up the entire hour, that would be beautiful. Tell me you got this."

I wanted to punch him in the face.

Jade sighed. "Yeah, I can do this." She turned to me. "You'll be close by, right?"

I nodded. It was killing me to put her in this position, especially after her meltdown back at the Dean's house. I knew this was weighing on her a lot more than she would ever admit. I took a moment to pull her into my arms and reassure her that I would never let anything bad happen to her again.

Patrick's phone dinged again, and he looked down at it just as the others arrived. Professor Jordan was with them this time, which surprised me. She walked with purpose carrying a gas can with her.

Before we realized what was happening, she started pouring the gas onto the dumpster, then stepped back and lit a match. I jumped in to stop her.

"What are you doing?" I demanded.

The match died out as she looked to the Dean for assistance.

"It's okay, Brett. She's on our side. She brought up a good point that people could start talking the second someone notices us all hanging out back here and we need to be as discreet as possible," he told me.

"How the hell is lighting a dumpster on fire being discreet?" That was the dumbest idea I'd heard yet, but I kept that last part to myself.

"It gives us a reason to be back here that the students won't question," she said calmly as she struck another match.

I was still standing between her and the dumpster when Patrick looked up.

"Bloody hell!" he swore. "Put the match down, now."

Professor Jordan's eyes shifted between Patrick and the match, then she looked at the dumpster. Somehow, I knew she wasn't going to listen to him. This was confirmed when she started to pull back her arm to launch the lit match into the extremely flammable dumpster. I reacted without thinking, grabbing her wrist and blowing out the match. She scrambled for a third one, but by then Patrick was on her, pinning her up against the wall and asking if anyone had anything to restrain restraining her.

"Stop it," she yelled, trying to draw attention to all of us. "You're hurting me," she tried instead.

"What is the meaning of this?" Dean Shannahan demanded. "Patrick, let her go. She's only trying to help. She's a trusted Verndari."

"Are you certain of that, Cormack?" he asked. "Because my intel says otherwise.

While restraining the professor, he passed his phone to the Dean. I chanced a look, and sure enough, a surveillance image of Professor Jordan in this exact spot was displayed. There was no doubt it was her.

"Hey, what's that in her hand?" I asked, pointing it out in the picture. "Looks like some sort of remote control?"

"Check her bag," Patrick said.

"No," she protested.

The bag had been abandoned while she had fought to set the dumpster on fire. Why would she do that? I kneeled down and examined the contents of her bag finding a similar item to what I saw in the picture. It was small, silver, not much bigger than a car remote. There was only one button on the thing. It wasn't labeled, but I tried pressing it. The brick wall moved. I held it down until the door was fully opened.

"What is the meaning of this?" Cormack demanded.

"I'm not saying another word," she spat.

Patrick searched her and tossed over another pack of matches and her cell phone.

"Why was she trying to set the dumpster on fire anyway?" I finally asked.

"Likely a signal. I know you thought you only had one Raglan here, Cormack, but looks like that was wrong. I'm calling in my team. Brett, take Jade to meet with Rodgers. Keep him occupied while we search the facility. This is the closet we've gotten to the Raglan in months. We can't afford to screw this up," Patrick said.

He quickly searched through his phone as we all watched. The Dean and Coach Meyers were clearly shocked to find Professor Jordan was in on it. That didn't sit well with me. The Verndari may be mostly good people, but it was clear to me they didn't have their house in order. Besides, there was always a fine line between friend and enemy. Some would say that Jade and I were a perfect example of that.

"I'm confident she didn't have time to warn anyone. There're no texts, emails, nothing. She'll never admit it, but I strongly suspect that was what the fire was for, a silent warning to everyone she's working with to get out."

"So we're safe to proceed?" I asked, needing that verbal confirmation.

"Yup. Jade, you're up."

Jade

Chapter 25

The last thing I wanted to do was meet face-to-face with Professor Rodgers, but I understood the importance of this meeting. Learning there were more than just him involved had shaken me, but I wasn't entirely shocked either.

If that nightmare truly had been a memory, then his lab was extensive and would have taken a lot of work to set up and keep hidden from everyone at the ARC. It was more than a two-man job even, but I wasn't ready to allow myself to even think about that.

Brett, Chase, and Jenna stayed far enough behind that we hoped Rodgers didn't notice them or think anything odd of them being in the café. At that hour, it wasn't very likely. The realization that Professor Jordan was in on everything had delayed us.

The second I walked into the café I spotted him sitting alone in the far corner. I quickly walked over sounding as frazzled as I felt and immediately began apologizing.

"I'm so sorry for being late, Professor. It's been a crazy morning and I just lost track of time, but I'm here now," I said and even managed a convincing smile. I looked down and noticed he didn't have any food yet. "Are you not eating? I'm starving," I rambled.

He relaxed and smiled back at me. "Relax Jade. I have an hour. We'll get some lunch then you can fill me in on what exactly I signed up for."

I nodded but couldn't talk. In all the chaos that had ensued, I hadn't had time to prepare for this. I had no idea what I was going to say that wouldn't tip him off. I took a deep breath, said a quick prayer and headed in the direction of food. A quick assessment told me that as usual, the pizza line was the longest, slowest line possible. I suddenly had a huge craving for pizza.

It took almost twenty minutes to get through the line and pay for my food. Rodgers had been back to the table for a while, eaten half his tray already, and was starting to look a little irritated.

I dropped my tray down across from his and he jolted in surprise. He had been distracted by his phone. I wish I knew what he was doing, or more importantly if anyone had tipped him off. The fact that he was still there told me that it was unlikely. I had to trust that Patrick had everything under control. I knew they were all counting on me.

On my way back to the table I'd passed Brett and the rest of the crew. He'd nodded as I went by and looked proud and reassuring. Just knowing he was here helped calm my nerves. I glanced down at my watch. It was already twelve thirty. I was halfway through this nightmare and we hadn't even started the conversation yet.

Rodgers had barely looked up from his phone, and I was certainly in no hurry to talk, so I sat quietly. My hands were sweating from nerves and I kept having to wipe them on my jeans, but I thought I was doing a good job of looking calm and collected.

I slowly ate while Rodgers started looking more and more irritated, and that scared me. I had hazy memories of him losing his temper in the lab. I sensed he was close.

"I'm sorry Jade, but something's come up. I'm afraid we're going to have to reschedule," he said and started to stand. I still had twenty minutes left and needed to stall him.

"I'm sorry too, Professor. My first class is in twenty minutes and I'm not done until nine tonight. I don't think we'll have time before the challenge in the morning to discuss the event, so just plan accordingly. Brett has chosen his champion but he's keeping it very secretive so I'm not sure I'll be much help to you on strategy anyway, but I'm sure you'll do fine. I mean coyotes are amongst the most conniving, the strongest, and of course the smartest, so yours will do great. I'm certain of it. I wouldn't have chosen you otherwise," I said sweetly.

I amazed myself with how normal I sounded despite my rising panic over him leaving. And I knew the second I'd grabbed his attention. He paled and sat back down, setting his phone to the side. I looked down at it, noting it was now twelve forty-five. I could do this for a few more minutes.

"What do you mean my coyote will do great?" he asked.

"You know," I said. "In the coyote challenges tomorrow."

"You said we'd settle things the coyote way," he said. "I thought you meant a battle of wits, not an actual battle."

"Professor, are you feeling well?" I asked. "We all know the coyote way is a battle of strength. Sure, wits will help you through it, but it's the strongest animal that wins." I laughed and shook my head. "I'm sorry, I almost thought you were serious. I know you're just messing with me. I mean you're a coyote too, right? Of course you know this. Don't worry, you're going to do fine. Knowing Brett, he's probably picked a wolf, and we both know that even though he may be bigger and stronger, coyotes are faster and more calculating. I have no doubt you'll blindside him."

Just like I'm about to blindside you, I thought, smiling in a way he would think I was being reassuring.

The buzzer on my phone went off signaling five minutes to class. I grabbed my slice of pizza that I'd been unable to eat sooner and devoured it.

"That was my warning to get to class. I'm over in your building. We can talk on the way," I said cheerily, determined not to let him out of my sight until he was safely in front of his class. Afterall, Patrick said I should try to give them as much time as possible in the lab.

I was almost giddy as I disposed of the remainder of my food and waited for Rodgers. He was back to checking his phone. I suspected he was on the verge of bolting, but I was determined.

The second we stepped outside, I started talking. I ignored his irritation and rudely talked over him anytime he tried to interrupt or excuse himself as we walked across campus. I rambled on about how proud I was that he was willing to battle personally for my inclusion campaign, and I made up some bullshit time and place for the event. I acted completely oblivious to the fact he was trying to ditch me and stayed glued to his side, even correcting our course when he tried to veer off towards the science building.

"Um, professor? We're this way," I said.

I even escorted him right up to his classroom door. Much to my surprise, Violet and Kaitlyn were in his one o'clock class. They interceded the second he arrived, peppering him with assignment questions.

I wanted to squeal, but that would have drawn too much attention. I just knew Brett had somehow gotten word to Kaitlyn. There was no way that was a coincidence. The timing couldn't have been more perfect.

The right thing to do would have been to head to my own class, but there was no way I could sit through a lecture while wondering what was going on. When I was certain Rodgers was settled into his class and the coast was clear, I changed course and headed back to the alley behind the science center.

As I rounded the corner, an arm snuck out and grabbed me. I screamed out in fear.

"Woah, Jade, calm down. It's just me," Brett said.

My heart was already pounding in my chest even as relief flooded me. I threw my arms around him.

"It's okay. Sorry, I didn't mean to scare you. I should have known better."

"I'm okay, just a bit jumpy, but I did it! I actually did it! Did you text Kaitlyn for that handoff?"

He laughed. "Yeah. Did it work? She doesn't know anything, just that it was an important favor. I think she's a little pissy about that."

"Her and Violet both were brilliant! I don't think he's going anywhere for the next hour," I admitted.

"Aren't you supposed to be in class?" he asked.

I shrugged. "Did you really think I'd be able to sit through it with all this happening?"

Brett laughed. "No, that's why I held back. I also knew you'd be curious, but I want you to really consider if going in there is right for you."

I leaned in gave him a quick kiss. "I know you're worried about me, but I have to do this, Brett. I need to know with certainty that my dream was real."

He sighed and nodded in resolution. "I suspected as much. Come on."

When we reached the dumpster, the hidden door was closed. I gave Brett a concerned look.

He just smiled back and pulled out his phone. "Too conspicuous to leave it open."

Seconds after he hit send, the door clicked open. I took a deep breath and followed him inside. Fear crept in as he closed the door behind us.

"No way out," I sighed, trying to get a grip on my panic. We were standing at the top of a dark staircase. It all felt entirely too familiar.

"I'm here," Brett whispered as his hand rested on my lower back.

There was a light at the bottom of the staircase, so I crept down in that direction. The humming from the data center made my skin prick. The stairs spilled out into a hallway. I took the lead, peeking into a few rooms that looked like nothing more than storage.

By the third room like this, I got curious and walked in. Brett tried to stop me.

"The lab is down at the end of this hallway," he said.

I nodded but pushed into the room anyway. There were boxes piled everywhere, and they weren't dusty like you'd expect in an old storage room. It instantly reminded me of the archives at the law firm I'd worked for over the summer.

I stopped and pulled out the first box. It was filled with files. I chose one and opened it. My breath hitched in my throat. It was a very old file, and it contained documented details of a wolf pack in Bulgaria. It was dated back to the seventeen hundreds.

"Not good," I whispered.

"What? I'm sure they're just old school files," Brett said as he stood awkwardly at the door ready to move on.

"Not unless the school was around in the eighteenth century in Bulgaria," I said.

"What?" he asked, his interested finally piqued.

I pulled out another one. "This is a herd of elephants in Africa. It's only a few years old. Brett, I think these are all documented shifters throughout history. Do you have any idea how dangerous this information would be in the wrong hands?"

He opened a newer looking box near the door and gulped. "It's their research notes too, Jade."

I walked over and snatched it from him needing to see it with my own eyes.

"This is the third room full of these boxes that we've passed. It's like an entire shifter archive."

He reached for his phone.

"Who are you calling?" I asked, still not certain who we could and couldn't trust.

"Patrick. These files need to either be destroyed or in the hands of someone who won't abuse them."

I nodded. "You trust him?"

"With my life," he said. "Patrick? Dude, we have a huge problem and I'm not sure who to trust here. Did your guys make it in?"

"Silas just called and said they were parking. What is it Brett?" I could hear Patrick say.

"I need you to excuse yourself, tell them you're letting your team in or something and head for the stairs."

They hung up and Patrick never once questioned Brett. We looked out the small window in the door and waited to ensure he was alone before making our presence noticed.

"In here," Brett whispered after cracking the door open.

"What's going on?" Patrick asked.

Brett looked at me and nodded.

I took a deep breath. "Everyone seems to have bypassed these front rooms while looking for the lab, but Patrick, there's a goldmine of information in here. I'm talking thousands of years of documented data on shifters."

"You're serious?" he asked.

Brett handed him the first file I'd read. His eyes widened as he scanned it.

"Bloody hell! No way am I handing all this over to the Verndari."

"Didn't expect you would," Brett said. "That's why we called you."

Patrick grabbed his phone. "Archie, I need you to line us up several shipping cargo containers and trucks to carry them. This is of the utmost priority. Christmas is coming early for you son, and I can't think of anyone on this Earth that would appreciate it more."

"Who's Archie?" I asked Brett.

"Hell if I know, but if Patrick thinks this is a good idea, then I do too."

When Patrick was finally done making several calls, we asked him what was going on.

"What are you going to do with all this stuff?" Brett asked.

"Archie's working on a secluded holding facility. He'll personally oversee the information contained here. Trust me on this, there is no one else more qualified. Bring Jade on out to Westin sometime and I'll introduce you both and show you a bit of what I've been up to. I'd say you've both earned that right."

The next call Patrick got was his team arriving. I got a glimpse of Silas. He was huge and scary looking. He and his team looked like a pack of military elite forces. Not someone you'd want to mess with.

With them guarding Patrick's back we all headed for the lab.

I sucked in a sharp breath when I entered the room. It was exactly as I'd seen in my dream. I took a couple deep breaths willing myself not to hyperventilate. The sounds, the smells, the layout was all spot on.

Brett never left my side.

"Are you okay?" he kept asking me every few minutes.

"No, I'm not," I finally confessed. "But I will be. I need to be here now."

I walked over to the cages lining the far wall and looked up.

Brett growled behind me in understanding. I started to break down a little and turned to hide in his chest. It didn't take long before Ember noticed and came over. She hugged me even though I never let go of Brett. Chad followed Ember's lead. Chase and Jenna somehow ended up in our big group hug too.

"You're tough, Jade. I can tell. You're going to be okay," Chase said.

"And when you're not, it's okay to lean on your mate," Jenna added.

"I'm sorry you guys. It's just hard to be here," I admitted. I pointed up to the top cage above us. "That's where they kept me. I was here for three days and no one missed me. What does that say about me?"

"That you were lonely," Ember said. "I know that feeling. I was too, before I found Chad. You have Brett now, Jade. You never have to be alone again."

I looked up at my mate as he smiled and nodded. "She's right about that. After seeing this place, I'm going to have to change all my classes to match yours because there's no way in hell you'll be leaving my sight anytime soon, and I don't give a damn what anyone around campus has to say about it. It's not just because you're my mate and it's my job to protect you—it's because I'm falling crazy in love with you and want to protect you."

I blushed furiously as he'd just announced that in front of his friends. He smiled as he leaned down to kiss me. For the first time in my life, I truly felt loved.

Brett

Epilogue

Patrick brought in several additional resources to clean out the basement and ensure all the files we found were secured. Everyone readily admitted that if it hadn't been for Jade, they would have overlooked all of it.

Professor Rodgers showed up after his final class that day and was taken by surprise. He tried to plead innocence like he didn't know anything about what was going on and someone was trying to set him up. Unfortunately for him, Patrick's team had surveillance footage of him coming and going from the hidden doorway regularly, including pictures of him carrying Jade on the night she was kidnapped.

The Verndari assured us that they had facilities already in place to deal with people like him and Professor Jordan, and they would not be seeing the light of day anytime soon. A notice went out the next week that they'd resigned due to personal issues.

Those of us that were in the know were content with the outcome but still on edge. The Raglan lab was shut down and the two biggest culprits were in custody and being dealt with. However, Patrick had confided in me the need to remain diligent, as he and his team strongly believed that there was no way only two people put together that place and maintained it. They had to have had help, but for the moment the worst of the threat was gone.

Patrick and his team would spend the next several weeks at the ARC cleaning up the mess. When the time came, I was sad to see him go. He was definitely one of the good guys.

But well before that, and before Chase and Jenna headed back home, we had one epic open Row party!

* * * * *

"After everything that went down yesterday, I just don't know if I'm up for this," Jade whined.

"Babe, you have to come. This is your party," I reminded her.

She pouted. "This is not my party. This is the party you arranged as a means to belittle me and my cause. Plus, you do realize that by calling me "babe" you're setting the feminist movement back like fifty years."

She loved when I called her that, and nothing she could say would convince me otherwise, because every time I did, her eyes sparkled.

"Who cares why it started in the first place. After yesterday I get it. We're all in this together. Shifters need to unite," I said.

She snorted. "You can't actually tell anyone that."

"I can tell you and really does anyone else matter?"

She sighed. "Flattery will get you everywhere in life."

"Will it get me in your pants? Cause we have a good fifteen minutes before we absolutely have to head out."

She laughed. I loved that sound. I loved her.

"Are you trying to admit you're just a two-pump chump then?

I feigned hurt, holding my hand over my heart. "You of all people should know better, and if last night didn't prove that point, then forget the party, I've got work to do."

I walked over and tried to wrap my arms around her intending to kiss her and not let things escalate further than that—probably.

She pushed me away laughing some more. "Behave," she warned.

"Then you'll go to the party?" I asked.

Jade rolled her eyes. "Do I have a choice?"

"Technically yes, and technically no."

"Explain," she said as she got up and moved to the mirror to fix her makeup for the evening.

I laid back on my bed and watched already knowing I'd won this battle.

"First, you always have a choice, but I've sworn not to let you out of my sight, remember? And I have to at least make an appearance tonight and give a speech, so you need to be in my view during that time. So, if you want to leave afterwards, fine. It'll be hard on me, but I will make the best of it, if you force the issue. I suppose it wouldn't be the end of the world if I had to be locked up in here with you all night long."

I was being over-the-top dramatic, but I knew it was entertaining her.

"I'm ready, already," she said.

I grinned and jumped up to kiss her. "We've worked really hard on this. I think you're going to be impressed by how serious we took this party and how well all seven houses worked together."

"Are you still worried I'm going to crash your party?" she teased. At least I hoped she was teasing.

"No, of course not. I'm just telling you that it may have started as a way to get back at you, but that's not what it's about tonight."

"You're right," she said, giving me a quick kiss before opening the door and heading out to join the party.

The doghouse was empty as everyone was already outside. You could hear the music pumping and feel the energy before we even reached the door. I grabbed her by the waist and stole one final kiss. She was still adamant that we keep our mating a secret for now, but the guys were right, it was going to be really hard in a crowd of unmated males even though we had already bonded. My coyote was just too on edge with everything we'd faced over the last forty-eight hours.

Once we joined the party, Jade immediately found Kaitlyn and their friends Melissa and Violet. I hated her being out of arm's reach. I knew we were safe from Rodgers and Jordan being held in custody, but I couldn't help fear that there were still more out there. Only time would tell but those thoughts didn't sit well with my coyote, who kept trying to surge anytime I walked too far away from Jade.

She did look happy though as she laughed and even danced with her girlfriends. I had to remember to thank Kaitlyn for keeping an eye out for her. As if she had just read my thoughts, Kaitlyn looked up from across the way and smiled at me. She gave a quick nod as if to say, "I got her back, you don't have to worry." Then she went back to dancing.

Time flew as I made my rounds, doing my thing, and checking to make sure everything was running smoothly. It felt like every student at the ARC had shown up and was having a great time. It was safe to say this party would go down in ARC history as a huge success and I really owe it all to Jade. Without her pressure about being more inclusive around campus, I never would have suggested an all-campus, open Row party, and then I might have missed out on finding my one true mate, too.

I laughed to myself. It was hard to believe how much my life had changed in just one week.

Chad walked with a stiff smile on his face. "Ayanna sent me to tell you that according to the schedule, you're two minutes late on giving your welcome speech."

"The schedule? Dude this is a party."

"Yeah, but you're the genius who thought Tiffany and Ayanna working together was a good idea. I think they may actually become friends from this." Chad shuddered. "Terrifying thought! Now get up on that stage before they come looking for you, and let me just say, that clipboard of hers is scary."

I laughed but headed to the stage. It was hard to believe this time next year I'd be leaving this legacy to Chad. I knew he was up for the job. What I didn't know was where I'd be or what life would look like. I planned to have a long talk with Jade about that soon. If she was serious about not staying at the ARC for grad school, I needed to get some applications sent in ASAP, because the one thing I was absolutely certain of was, that I would follow that crazy woman anywhere.

From my perch on the stage Lambda Beta Pi put together at Tiffany's demand, I searched the crowd before me for Jade. Kaitlyn and their friends were right up front, but Jade was nowhere to be found. I fought down the panic trying to set in and launched into my prepared speech.

"Welcome Warriors! Hope you guys are having a great time tonight. I know most of you are here to see what I'll do this week," I paused at the roar of laughter. Grinning, I continued. "But I promise to keep a sober head. For the last few months, Jade Michaels has launched a campaign for inclusion. Now, I know what most of you are thinking, that she launched a campaign against Greek Row, and at first I felt that way, too, but the truth is that she opened my eyes to realize that here on Greek Row, all we really want is inclusion, to feel like we're a part of something, to not be alone. Because of this, we stand here united today, all seven houses at once for the very first time in ARC history and partying it up with each and every one of our fellow students, and it's awesome! So for those of you that didn't come here to see if I'd get drunk and crowd surf naked again, but to see how Jade would retaliate, I'm sorry to disappoint you, but we've called a truce, so going forward we will be working together instead of against each other."

I expected some sort of reaction from that, but I guessed I stunned them into silence. Then I felt her. The hair on the back of my neck stood up and I knew without turning around that Jade had just walked onto my stage. Was this how she had felt standing before everyone when I did that and we'd both been blindsided by the mating call? It was worse than naked crowd surfing.

Out of the corner of my eye I saw her step forward and wave to the crowd. I chanced a look over and grinned, shaking my head.

"Or maybe not?" I asked into the mic as our audience erupted in laughter.

Jade opened her hand and I laughed as I passed her the mic.

"How's everybody doing tonight?" she asked and had every person there cheering. "As many of you know, last weekend's bonfire got a little weird, even for me." I shook my head when they laughed. She had them eating out of the palm of her hand, and I couldn't have been prouder. "What you guys don't know is why. And I promise you it is absolutely nothing like any of you have imagined. See when I was standing on that stage talking to you all last weekend, something crazy and unbelievable happened. I found my one true mate."

A chorus of "awe" rang out and my heart soared. Was she really doing what I thought she was doing?

"Let me tell you, that is not something I'd wish on anyone either. Not the finding him part." She rolled her eyes dramatically. "That part was kind of cool, but the part of doing it front of a thousand people was horrifying. Neither of us handled it very well. I ran and hid the second I got off that stage. While he got completely shitfaced, crowd surfed naked, and from what I heard, started a new campus tradition of flying tacos."

Half the crowd was stunned silent as her words sunk in, the others immediately began whispering about us. I just grinned from ear to ear and shrugged happily.

"Trust me, no one could be more shocked than the two of us!" she added. That seemed to break through the stupor that had settled in and everyone laughed.

I decided to take the opportunity and publicly claim her too. I stepped forward, ready to kiss my mate, but she put her hand on my chest and pushed back.

"Not so fast," she said in the mic. "See, Brett here thinks that in light of our, well, situation, that all is forgiven. But let's be real you guys. Payback's a bitch!"

Before I knew what was happening, the DJ queued up "Fate" by Our Last night and Jade shoved the microphone into my hands and dove off the stage with a battle cry. My heart leapt into my throat as I tried to stop her, but right up front were all my brothers carefully passing her off and watching closely as she crowd surfed around.

Kaitlyn yelled out to me. "Brett!"

I looked down to find her.

"Got you!" she screamed, pointing at me and laughing.

I shook my head and laughed.

"Enjoy the party everyone!" I said into the mic, and then got off the stage quickly to go get my feisty mate! I'm even thinking that some more payback is in order, only during our private time later. My coyote liked that idea and then howled in agreement!

Dear Reader,

I truly hope you enjoyed Brett and Jade's story. They were a lot of fun to write and took a few twists and turns even I didn't see coming. If you loved it as much as I loved writing it, do me a favor and drop me a review!

For further information on my books, events, and life in general, I can be found online here:

Website: www.julietrettel.com

Facebook: http://www.facebook.com/authorjulietrettel

Facebook Fan Group:
https://www.facebook.com/groups/compounderspod7/

Instagram: http://www.instagram.com/julie.trettel

Twitter: http://www.twitter.com/julietrettel

Goodreads:
http://www.goodreads.com/author/show/14703924.Julie_Trettel

BookBub: https://www.bookbub.com/authors/julie-trettel

Amazon: http://www.amazon.com/Julie_Trettel/e/B018HS9GXS

Join my newsletter! http://eepurl.com/cwRHij

Much love and thanks,
Julie Trettel

Check out more great books by Julie Trettel!

The Compounders Series

The Compounders: Book1
http://www.amazon.com/dp/B018HKIU7O/?tag=kp-jtret-20

DISSENSION
http://www.amazon.com/dp/B01N6FSGLE/?tag=kp-jtret-20

DISCONTENT
http://www.amazon.com/dp/B07215QYL1/?tag=kp-jtret-20

SEDITION
http://www.amazon.com/dp/1624870678/?tag=kp-trettel-20

Westin Pack

One True Mate
https://www.amazon.com/dp/B071HXL3R2

Fighting Destiny
https://www.amazon.com/dp/B07575HC9T

Forever Mine
https://www.amazon.com/dp/B077V9WHMG

Confusing Hearts
https://www.amazon.com/dp/B07BP9XL9W

Can't Be Love
https://www.amazon.com/dp/B07DCCRB58

Under a Harvest Moon (prequel)
https://www.amazon.com/dp/B07TVL1CRZ

Collier Pack

Breathe Again
https://www.amazon.com/dp/B07F6KN6G3/

Run Free
https://www.amazon.com/dp/B07KFNY1DH/

In Plain Sight
https://www.amazon.com/dp/B07P5J1NCF/

Broken Chains
https://www.amazon.com/dp/B07RL5R4XZ

ARC Shifters

Pack's Promise
https://www.amazon.com/dp/B07J5455XG

Winter's Promise
https://www.amazon.com/dp/B07MBXM36R

About the Author

Julie Trettel is author of The Compounders, Westin Pack, Collier Pack, and ARC Shifters Series. She comes from a long line of story tellers. Writing has always been a stress reliever and escape for her to manage the crazy demands of juggling time and schedules between work and an active family of six. In her "free time," she enjoys traveling, reading, outdoor activities, and spending time with family and friends.

Visit
www.JulieTrettel.com

47741002R00103